MW01004873

THE CATCH
and Other War Stories

Kenzaburō Ōe
Haruo Umezaki
Tamiki Hara
Fumiko Hayashi

Selected and Introduced by
Shōichi Saeki

KODANSHA INTERNATIONAL LTD.
Tokyo, New York & San Francisco

Originally published by Kodansha International Ltd. under the title *The Shadow of Sunrise* (with one additional story).

Published by Kodansha International Ltd., 12–21 Otowa 2-chome, Bunkyo-ku, Tokyo 112 and Kodansha International /USA Ltd., 10 East 53rd Street, New York, New York 10022 and 44 Montgomery Street, San Francisco, California 94104. Printed in Japan.

LCC 80–84420
ISBN 0–87011–457–3
JBC 0093–789387–2361

First paperback edition, 1981

Table of Contents

Introduction

The four stories printed in this book share one common theme—the impact of the Pacific War (1941–45) on the Japanese mind. Purists might complain of the absence of battle scenes in this volume. There are no blood-and-thunder descriptions of fighting, no naval engagements, no jungle fire fights, no dismembered hands hanging from barbed wire.

It is true that none of these short stories is a pure "war story" in the strict sense of the term. Together, however, they compose a fugue based on the war and its aftermath. They are stories of human events that only occur during and as a result of that overwhelmingly inhuman event called war. And though ultimately and universally human, they are at the same time intrinsically Japanese.

The aim of this collection is to present a spectrum of human situations in wartime, with the proviso that the standard scorched-earth muddy-foxhole drama is readily available on magazine racks or at least once weekly during the prime mid-evening TV viewing time. The emphasis is on tracing the war's impact on people, not on representing a theater of war. And, being limited in terms of space, we felt obliged to forego a comprehensive picture of the Japanese reaction for a few compelling, typical examples.

Literature, by definition, goes beyond the psychological case history, and though each of these stories is in its own way a personal record, they all belong to the realm of literature. Our selection was based on the principle that each must be enjoyable as a story, while providing a variety of locales, of characters, and individual responses.

All the stories in this book were written after the war. Umezaki's "Sakurajima" was published in 1946, immediately following the war, and Hara's "Summer Flower" appeared in 1947. Hayashi's "Bones" was written in 1948, and Ōe's "The Catch" in 1958. Reading these four in their chronological order of publication, a noticeable difference in the tone of each story, in the attitudes of the central characters and of the writers themselves, should be apparent.

The narrator-hero of "Sakurajima," being a petty officer in the navy, is a direct participant, however passive and reluctant, in the military war effort. We feel he is emotionally involved in the war, however aloof and detached he pretends to be. It is already July 1945 when the story begins, and Japan's impending defeat is in the air. He knows that the landing of U.S. forces is a far from distant reality: "... I became acutely conscious of something unseen tightening its ring around me and hemming me in." Though the story starts with the hero indulging in the common excesses of drink and a night with a prostitute, on the whole his responses are subdued. Being oppressed with a sense of ever-approaching death, he tries to acclimatize to its "tightening ring" instead of reacting to it in a violent way. There are no emotional outbursts, no violent conflicts. The tone of the story as a whole is reserved.

The author, Haruo Umezaki (1915–65), served in the navy and was stationed at several naval bases on the southernmost main island, Kyushu, during the latter part of the war. He admitted he drew largely on his own experiences of those years in writing "Sakurajima." This is a story intensely personal both in tone and content, an invitation to share those gloomy days of early summer, 1945.

For Umezaki, there was no exit from his situation. He refused to pay lip service to the ultra-patriotic ideas promulgated in wartime Japan, yet could not believe in the value of his own individual rebellion. With nothing to depend upon, he felt an acute helplessness and isolation. But he resisted the temptation to indulge a sentimental nihilism, concentrating instead on a detailed examination of concrete circumstances.

Refraining from developing the potentially dramatic conflict between the authoritarian C.P.O. Kira and the narrator, Umezaki presents us with several ominously vivid scenes and images serving as "objective correlatives" for the inner state of the hero. "The frighteningly pale moon," the prostitute with one ear, an old, enfeebled farmer who fails in an attempt to hang himself—these images are all, as it were, inner landscapes imbued with the deep personal emotion of the hero. C.P.O. Kira, in whom the demands of the Japanese war machine are personified, assumes the force of a pervading shadowy grotesque who somehow encompasses and defines the whole psychic landscape of war, and against whom any open struggle can only mean self-defeat and contradiction in suicidally opposing the very force that demands one's suicide. In Umezaki, the desire for life meant rejecting even opposition to those forcing one to fight—an inner conflict that focuses attention on the dark highlights of a world alive with sight and sound.

"Summer Flower" by Tamiki Hara (1905–51) is even more personal than "Sakurajima." Indeed, it is almost straight autobiography, rather than fiction. The author was living in Hiroshima when the atomic bomb was dropped on the city on August 6, 1945. He simply relates what happened to him on that fatal day and the following days. He neither comments nor moralizes; he just reports. This restraint is all the more remarkable for the intensity and indescribable horror of that experience. The memory of that fatal moment may indeed have been instrumental in Hara's tragic suicide four years after the publication of "Summer Flower."

Here again we encounter that impressive combination of an intense personal experience and a deliberately reserved, almost reticent manner of narration. I do not want to claim a monopoly of this approach for Japanese writers, but it seems to form an essential part of the Japanese literary heritage: emphasis on the personal aspect of experience, on the one hand, and a preference, on the other, for dealing with it through compressed, implicit imagery.

"Bones" by Fumiko Hayashi (1904–51), the only woman novelist represented in this anthology, belongs to a more conventional type of short story: a war widow taking to the streets—the theme seems almost too trite. But the heroine of "Bones" is hardly a passive victim, a mechanical doll used to prove some kind of simple determinism. She is thoroughly a victim of war and her country's defeat, but one senses a certain desperate vitality in her. She is crushed by circumstances, by the shifting forces of the times, but at the same time a unique feminine vitality begins to emerge and assert itself. Her faithfulness to herself and to her dead husband is sacrificed, but she is awakened as a woman, and recovers a sort of self-confidence, however desperate. Astonishingly, she seems to gain more than she loses—a fact that is both horrifying and life-affirming. The subtle change wrought in her by her ordeal is described with a vivid, delicate touch, and her personal response to pain has a convincing reality about it.

Kenzaburō Ōe (1935–) was only six when the war broke out, and there is a sense of aesthetic distance in "The Catch"; it is not so much a personal record as a product of the imagination, a successful evocation of the sensuous world of the grade-school boy. Ōe's style is remarkable for the freedom with which he uses metaphor—unusual in most Japanese writers, who employ this literary device sparingly and with great circumspection. Ōe sometimes seems to enjoy playing with metaphors for their own sake, but in "The Catch" his richly metaphorical style corresponds effectively to the acute, sensuous, and playful sensibility of the village boys.

One Japanese critic spoke of its "mischievous inhumanity" when this story won the Akutagawa Prize. The remark applied not only to Ōe's style but to his attitude as a novelist. The "catch" is a black American pilot caught and imprisoned by some villagers, and looked on and treated as a strange animal; the boys of the village are particularly excited by their prize. But this is a story of initiation, and the point of the tale lies in the development of a human relationship between these boys and the captive airman. Neglected, left to their own devices by the village adults, the children learn this process for themselves, and an intimacy develops between these "aliens" and the alien in their midst. At the very moment of communion, however, the "catch" is killed, and the boys stand awestruck. Their initiation is double-edged, a discovery not only of the possibilities of human relationships, but of the evil inherent in human society.

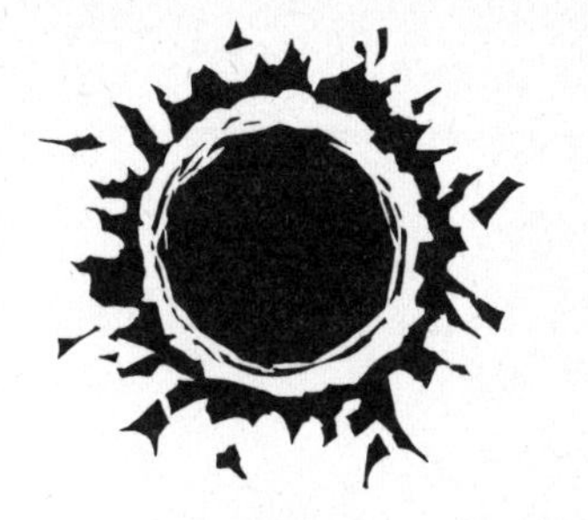

Kenzaburō Ōe

The Catch

MY YOUNG BROTHER AND I were at the temporary crematory at the bottom of the valley, the rudimentary crematory that had been made, quite simply, by cutting a space in the dense shrubs and spading up a shallow layer of earth. We were scratching about with pieces of wood in the soft surface earth that smelled of fat and ashes. Already the bottom of the valley was submerged in sunset and a mist cold as underground water gushing out in a wood. A light the color of grapes was pouring down on the small village, built along a cobbled road on the hillside facing the valley, where we lived. I straightened my bent back and gave a capacious, languid yawn. My brother stood up too, yawned briefly, and smiled at me.

We gave up our collecting and, hurling the pieces of wood into the depths of the lush summer grass, set off with arms about each other's shoulders up the path to the village. We had gone to the crematory to look for any well-shaped bones still remaining that could be used for badges to wear on our chests, but they had all been gathered already by the village children, and we found absolutely nothing. It seemed I should have to beat one of my primary-school friends into handing over his. I remembered how, two days before, I had peered between a black row of grown-up legs and seen a dead woman from the village being cremated, lying there in the light of the flames with an expression full of sadness and her naked, mounded belly upturned to the sky. I felt scared. Grasping my brother's thin arm, I quickened my pace. Once more I seemed to smell in my nostrils the smell of the dead, that smell that reminded me of the sticky excretion emitted by some beetles if we clenched them tight in our fingers.

Our village had been forced into cremating its dead in the open by the protracted rainy season that had preceded that summer, when the long, persistent rains had continued till floods were a daily occurrence. A landslide had smashed down the suspension bridge that was a shortcut from our village to the town, closing our village's branch of the local primary school, bringing mail to a standstill, and obliging the village grown-ups who must go to town to wind their way along the narrow, insecure path along the ridge of the hills. To carry dead to the crematorium was out of the question.

Yet for our village, which had been built to open up new land in the area and was old without being fully grown, to be completely cut off from the town was no serious hardship. The townsfolk despised us as if we were unclean animals; as for us, all our daily needs were crammed within the small huddle of houses on the slope looking down on the narrow valley. It was the beginning of summer, too, and we children were only too pleased that our branch of the local school should be shut.

Where the cobbled road began at the entrance to the village, Harelip was standing with a dog in his arms. My hand pressed on my brother's shoulder, I ran through the deep shadow cast by the old apricot trees to peer at the dog in Harelip's arms.

"Hey, look here!" said Harelip, jogging the puppy in his arms till it growled. The arm he thrust out towards me was covered with bites crusted around with blood and dog hairs. On his chest and at the nape of his short, thick neck, the bite marks stood out like buds. "Look!" he repeated solemnly.

"You broke your promise to go wild-dog catching with me," I said, choking with surprise and mortification. "You went alone, didn't you?"

"I called for you," said Harelip hastily, "but you weren't in, so. . . ."

"You sure got bitten," I said, tickling the puppy with the tip of my finger. Its nostrils were distended, and its eyes savage as a wolf's. "Did you crawl into the nest?"

"I wound a leather belt round my neck first, so they couldn't get at my throat," he said in a voice full of pride.

In the twilight purple of the hillsides and the cobbled roadway, I could clearly see Harelip, armed with the leather belt around his throat, getting bitten all over by the wild dogs as he crawled out of the nest of dried grass and shrubs with a puppy in his arms.

"It's all right as long as they don't get your throat," he said self-confidently. "Besides, I waited till the young'uns were left by themselves."

"Gee!" said my young brother dreamily.

"He's real used to me already," continued Harelip, overdoing the self-confidence. "He'll never go back to the other wild dogs now."

I and my brother remained silent.

"You watch!" he said, setting the dog down on the road and taking away his hands.

"Watch!"

But instead of looking down at the dog, we looked up at the sky that canopied the narrow valley. A plane of unbelievable size was crossing it at terrifying speed. For a few moments, our whole beings were pervaded by the mighty roar that filled and pulsed through the air. We stood, transfixed in the noise like winged insects trapped in oil.

"It's an enemy plane!" Harelip shouted. "The enemy's come!"

We stared up at the sky and shouted till we were hoarse. "Enemy plane. . . ."

But there was nothing in the sky any more save the

clouds brown-gleaming in the setting sun. When we came to ourselves again, Harelip's dog was bounding away yelping down the stony road. Scarcely had we noticed it when it had leapt into the woods and vanished, leaving Harelip open-mouthed, his body poised for pursuit. My brother and I laughed as though we were drunk, and Harelip himself, for all his mortification, could not repress a smile.

We left Harelip and ran back to where the storehouse squatted like some great beast in the twilight air. Father was in the dark, unfloored part, making preparations for our meal.

"We saw a plane!" my brother shouted at Father's back. "A great, big enemy plane." Father gave a grunt without turning round. I took Father's heavy shotgun down from the wooden wall, and putting it on my shoulder went arm in arm with my brother up the dark stairs.

"Pity the dog got away," I said.

"And the plane too," said my brother.

We lived in a small room once used for rearing silkworms, on the second floor of the communal storehouse in the center of the village. We had not a single piece of furniture to our name. Father's shotgun shone with a dull gleam, as though the wooden stock, with its oily luster, had been transformed into iron like the barrel, so hard that it numbed one's hand if one hit it. This gun gave a kind of focus to our humble home. It, and the dried weasel skins hanging in bundles from the bare beams, and traps of various kinds, were all we had. Father managed somehow to support us by shooting rabbits, birds and—in snowy winters—wild boar, and by drying the skins of the weasels he caught in his traps and selling them at the local town office.

As we polished the gun with an oily rag, my brother and I peered at the night sky through the gap in the wooden door, half expecting to hear once more the roar of an airplane. But it was very uncommon for an airplane to pass over our village. Putting the gun back on its wooden rack on the wall, we threw ourselves down on the bed, pressing our bodies together, to wait with growing pangs of hunger for Father to bring the pot of rice gruel with vegetables.

In the town beyond the rolling hills, the war that had gone on too long had become something vast and cumbersome, a legend that breathed its air of stagnation over everything. For us, however, the war meant nothing more than the absence of the young men from the village and an occasional announcement of death in battle delivered by the postman. Even the enemy planes that had begun of late to pass over the village were no more than a kind of rare bird.

Close to dawn, we were awakened by a heavy rumbling and a terrifying crash. I saw Father start half out of the blanket spread over his bed and crouch there, his eyes keen with desire, like a beast hidden in the night forest waiting to pounce on its prey. He did not pounce, though, but flopped down on the bed again and sank straight back into sleep.

I waited for a long time with ears cocked, but the rumbling did not come again. I waited patiently, quietly breathing the damp air with its smell of mildew and small animals, in the pale moonlight that crept through the lofty skylight of the storehouse. A long time had passed when suddenly my brother, asleep with sweaty forehead pressed against my side, gave a feeble sob. He, too, must have been waiting for the earth to rumble again, and the suspense had become too much for him. His neck as he lay there was thin and delicate as the stem of some plant; I pressed the palm of my hand against the nape, and gently rocked it to reassure him. Then, soothed by the gentle motion of my own arm, I too fell asleep.

When I awoke, the opulent morning light was surging in through every chink in the boards and it was already hot. Father was not there, nor was his gun on the wall. I shook my brother awake and we went out, still naked to the waist, into the road before the storehouse. A fierce morning light was beating down on the cobbles and the stone steps, dazzling the children out there in the open: children idly standing, children rolling their dogs over to pick out the fleas, children shouting as they chased each other about—but no adults. My brother and I ran to the blacksmith's under the great camphor tree, but there was no charcoal fire shooting forth its bright flames over the dusky earthen floor; there was no sound of the bellows, and there was no blacksmith, up to his waist in the earth, picking up the red-hot iron with his abnormally sunburnt, dried-up arm. Never before had we known the blacksmith not to be in his shop in the morning. Bare arms linked, we went back along the cobbled road in silence. In the whole village not a single adult was to be seen. The women were surely lurking somewhere in the gloomy depths of the houses. But here there were only the children, drowning in the flood of sunlight. A spasm of apprehension gripped my chest.

Harelip, who had been sprawled on the stone steps leading down to the spring where the village drew its water, caught sight of us and came running and waving. He was puffed up with self-importance, and sticky white flecks of saliva were blowing through the split in his lip.

"Hey, have you heard?" he shouted, banging me on the shoulder. "Have you heard?"

"Mm?" I said non-committally.

"That plane yesterday, it crashed in the hills during the night," he said. "They're looking for the enemy fliers who were on board. All the grown-ups have gone to hunt them with shotguns."

"Will they shoot 'em?" asked my young brother in a tense voice. "The enemy soldiers?"

"I don't expect they'll shoot them. What with the shortage of cartridges," he explained gratuitously. "It'd be better to catch them alive."

"I wonder what happened to the plane," I said.

"It went into the fir wood and smashed to bits," replied Harelip. He spoke rapidly, his eyes flashing. "The postman saw it. You know the place, don't you?"

I knew it. Just now, the fir flowers would be in bloom, like feathery ears of grass. By the end of summer, cones the shape of birds' eggs would have formed in their stead, waiting for us to go and collect them for ammunition, and at dusk and dawn in our storehouse the brown bullets would fly with sudden, sharp cracks.

"Well?" said Harelip, drawing his lips back to bare pinkly gleaming gums. "You know it, don't you?"

"Of course I know it," I said, pressing my lips together.

"Are you going?" Harelip peered at me with a cunning smile that wrinkled the skin round his eyes into innumerable folds. "If you're going I'll go and get my undershirt right away," I said, scowling at him. "You go on alone, I'll soon catch up with you."

Harelip's face crumpled up with pleasure. "No you don't," he said in a voice that could scarcely contain his satisfaction. "Children are forbidden to go into the hills. They might get shot by mistake for a foreign airman."

I dropped my head and stared at my feet with their short, sturdy toes pressed against the cobbles that burned in the morning sun. Disappointment welled up throughout my body as the sap wells up through a tree, bringing a flush to my skin that was warm like the guts of a freshly-killed chicken.

"I wonder what the enemy soldiers look like," my brother said.

We left Harelip and went back along the road, my arm round my brother's shoulders. Yes, I wondered, what did they really look like, and in what postures would they be hiding in the fields or the woods? Suddenly, it seemed that all the fields and woods about the village in the valley were filled with enemy soldiers, hiding with bated breath, and that the low sound of their breathing would at any moment swell into a terrifying clamor. Their sweaty skins and the pungent odor of their bodies lay heavy and inescapable over the whole valley.

"I hope they weren't dead," my young brother said dreamily. "I hope they bring them back alive."

The spittle stuck in our throats in the all-pervading sunlight, and hunger gnawed at the pits of our stomachs. In all likelihood Father would not be back till the evening: we should have to find food for ourselves. We went down to the well with the broken bucket behind the storehouse and drank, supporting ourselves by pressing our hands against the cold-sweating inner wall that bulged outward like the belly of a chrysalis. We drew water in a shallow iron basin, lit a fire, then thrust our arms into the chaff at the back of the storehouse and stole some potatoes. The potatoes as we washed them in cold water were hard as stones against the palms of our hands.

The meal that followed our brief labors was simple, but abundant. My brother, eating away like a happy animal at the potato clasped between his hands, was plunged in thought. "I wonder if the airmen are up fir trees," he said. "I saw a squirrel on a fir branch, you know."

"Mm.... The flowers are out on the firs, so it's a good place for hiding," I said.

"The squirrel too, it hid as soon as it saw me!" he said, smiling.

At this very moment, I reflected, the foreign airmen were lurking in the high branches of the fir trees, in the branches with flowers like fluffy heads of grass; and they were peering down through the clusters of fine green needles at my father and the others. The fir flowers sticking to the airmen's thick, padded flying suits made them look like squirrels that had fattened themselves for hibernation.

"Even if they hide in the trees the dogs'll find them and bark," my brother said confidently.

I waited, till clouds the color of a prairie fire flitted throughout the sky, till our valley was completely submerged in an ardent sunset, but still the grown-ups did not come back. I was beside myself with anticipation. The sunset had faded, a cool breeze that was good to the newly-burnt skin had sprung up from the valley, and the first shadows of evening had already crept into corners when, finally, the barking dogs and the grown-ups came back to a hushed village, to a village half-crazed with uneasy expectation. Running to meet them in a crowd of other children, I saw the great, black man who came surrounded by the grown-ups, and a sudden impact of fear set my head spinning.

The grown-ups encircled their catch. Lips solemnly compressed as when they went boar-hunting in the winter, they came walking towards us with bent backs, sadly almost. The catch himself wore, not the gray silk flying suit and black, tanned, leather flying boots, but a dark green jacket and trousers and heavy, clumsy shoes. He came dragging a lame leg, his large, gleaming black face turned up towards the last of the twilight. Around his ankles was fastened an iron chain from a boar trap, which set up a loud rattle as he walked. We children walked in an equally silent group, following the procession of grown-ups surrounding their catch. The procession proceded slowly as far as the open space in front of the branch school that served the village, then quietly came to a halt. I pushed my way through to the front of the group of children, but the old man who was headman of the village drove us away at the top of his voice. We retired beneath the clump of apricot trees in the corner of the open space, where we ensconced ourselves to survey the council of grown-ups through the ever-deepening dusk. The women stood in the entrances of the houses facing the open space, their arms folded beneath their white overalls. Their menfolk had come back with their catch from a dangerous expedition, and they strained to listen, impatient at the low voices in which the men were talking. Harelip gave me a vigorous poke in the ribs and led me apart from the other children, into the deep shadow beneath the camphor tree.

"He's a nigger, isn't he! I thought so from the start," he said in a voice trembling with excitement. "A real nigger!"

"Wonder what they'll do with him. Shoot him maybe," I said.

"Shoot him?" cried Harelip, his voice breathless with astonishment. "Shoot a real, live, genuine nigger?"

"But he's an enemy," I insisted without confidence.

"Enemy? Him an enemy?" he spluttered hoarsely, seizing me by the collar and spraying my whole face from the gap in his lip. "He's a nigger! Enemy, indeed!"

"Hey, hey!" My brother's voice came excitedly from the group of children. "Look at that!"

Harelip and I turned round and stared at the Negro airman. With drooping shoulders, he was urinating a short distance from the grown-ups, who looked on in embarrassment. His black body was gradually melting away into the deepening dusk, leaving only the dark green jacket and the trousers that looked like a workman's clothes. Head bent, he urinated at enormous length; then, just as a cloud of sighs rose from the watching children, he langorously shook his hips and finished.

The grown-ups once more encircled the Negro airman and slowly began to retrace their steps. We followed at a distance, in silent procession. The procession halted before the door at the side of the storehouse through which goods were loaded. Here, black as the entrance to some animal's lair, yawned the entrance to the cellar where every year we would store for the winter the best of the ripe autumn chestnuts, after killing the grubs under their skins with carbon disulfide. Impressively, as if it were the beginning of some ceremony, the grownups with the Negro in their midst sank into the opening, and a white flutter of grown-up arms shut the massive trapdoor from within.

Ears cocked, we watched the orange light that gleamed behind the narrow strip of cellar skylight exposed between the floor of the storehouse and the earth. We could not pluck up the courage actually to peep through the skylight, and the brief, uncertain period of waiting tired us immeasurably. Yet no shot rang out. Instead, the village headman's face peered out dimly from the half-opened trapdoor and bellowed at us, so that we were obliged to give up watching the skylight, even at a distance. But there was no complaint, and the children ran away along the cobbled road, their breasts swelling with the satisfying anticipation of night hours filled with bad dreams; and fear, summoned by their own loud footsteps, chased after them as they ran.

My young brother and I left Harelip hidden in the shadows of the apricot trees by the storehouse, still determined to observe the movements of the grown-ups and their catch, and went round to the front entrance of the storehouse. We climbed up to our dwelling in the loft, supporting ourselves as we went on the perennially damp handrail.

We were living, then, in the same house as the catch. However we pricked up our ears, of course, it was unlikely that any cry from the cellar could be heard in the loft. Even so, to be able to sit on one's bed on top of the cellar into which the Negro airman had been put was something splendid, adventurous and, for us, almost unbelievable. My teeth were chattering aloud with a mixture of excitement, terror, and pleasure, and my brother, with the blanket over his head and his knees drawn up, was trembling as though he had caught a bad cold. As we waited for Father to return, we smiled at each other in token of the good fortune that had suddenly befallen us.

We began to eat the hard, coldly sweating remains of the potatoes, not so much to soothe the pangs of hunger as to quell, by the rise and fall of our arms and the careful motions of our jaws, the turmoil in our breasts. Just then, Father came climbing up the stairs. Thrilling with anticipation, we watched him put his shotgun up on the rack and seat himself on the blanket spread on the bare floor, but he remained silent, merely glancing at the pot containing the potatoes we were eating. He's tired to death and irritable, I thought to myself. We were children, though, and could do nothing about it.

"Has the rice all gone?" Father asked. He stared at me, drawing his chin in till the stubble-covered skin beneath bulged out like a bag.

"Mm," I replied in a low voice.

"And the wheat, too?" He almost groaned with ill temper.

"Every bit gone," I said, growing irritable myself.

"What happened to the airplane?" my brother asked timidly.

"It caught fire. Nearly started a forest fire."

"Was it all burned up? Every bit?" asked my brother with a sigh.

"Only the tail left."

"The tail....!" he repeated rapturously.

"What happened to the others?" I asked. "Was he the only one on board?"

"Two other airmen were killed. He came down by parachute."

"Parachute...!" repeated my brother, increasingly enraptured. I took the plunge. "What are they going to do with him?" I asked.

"Feed him till we find out what they want to do with him in town."

"Feed him?" I asked, astonished. "Like an animal?"

"He's no better than a beast," Father declared solemnly. "Smells all over like a cow."

"I'd like to go and see him," said my brother, peering into Father's face, but Father went off down the stairs with sullen, set lips. I hugged my body in glee. We were keeping a Negro soldier! I could have thrown off my clothes and shouted it out loud. Keeping a Negro soldier like an animal....

The next morning Father shook me awake without speaking. It was just dawn. A mixture of strong sunlight and turbid gray mist crept in through every chink in the boards of the storehouse. I was still waking up as I busily gulped down my cold breakfast. Father, his gun on his shoulder and his lunch bundle tied round his waist, watched me eat my meal with eyes a muddy yellow from lack of sleep. Suddenly, I noticed that he was resting between his knees a tight roll of weasel skins, wrapped in a torn jute sack. I caught my breath–so he was going down to the town! He was almost certainly going to report to the office about the nigger.

A whirl of questions arose in my throat, threatening to delay my meal. But the way Father's muscular chin worked ceaselessly under its cover of coarse stubble told me that he was bad-tempered, his nerves on edge from lack of sleep. After his meal the night before, he had loaded his gun with fresh cartridges and gone out on night guard.

My brother was asleep, his head thrust beneath the blanket that smelled of moldy grass. Finishing my meal, I moved swiftly about on tiptoe so as not to wake him. I pulled my thick, dark green undershirt over my bare top half and put on the canvas running shoes that I never normally wore. Then I put the bundle from between Father's knees on my back and ran down the stairs.

Mist crept low along the damp road, and the whole sleeping village was wrapped in haze. The cocks had crowed themselves into silence, and not a dog barked. I saw a grown-up leaning against the apricot tree by the side of the storehouse with a gun in his hand. Father exchanged a few words with the guard. I darted a glance full of terror at the place, black as a wound, where the cellar skylight opened, half expecting the Negro's arm to come thrusting out to catch me. I wanted to get out of the village as quickly as possible. As we set out along the road, walking silently, and carefully lest we slip on the stones, the sun pierced the thick layer of mist and shed on us its warming, pertinacious rays.

"Are you going to the town to tell them about the nigger?" I inquired after my father's sturdy back.

"Uh?" grunted Father. "Oh, yes."

"Maybe a policeman'll come from the town station?"

"I don't know what will happen," growled Father. "Not till the report goes to the prefectural office."

"Why couldn't we go on looking after him in the village?" I said. "Maybe he's too dangerous?"

Father remained silent and unresponsive. I felt the

surprise and fear which I had experienced the night before, when they had brought the Negro airman to the village, reviving within my body. What was he doing now in the cellar? He would get out of the cellar, I was sure, slaughter all the people and the hunting dogs, and set fire to the houses. I trembled with fear, and did not want to think about it. I overtook Father and ran panting down the long slope.

It was lunchtime at the town office. We drank at the pump in the open square before the office, then seated ourselves for a long wait on a bench by a window through which the hot rays of the sun were beating. At last an old official, his lunch finished, came out and held a conversation in low tones with my father. Without more ado, the two disappeared into the mayor's office, whereupon I took the weasel skin to a counter where a number of small weighing machines stood. Here, the number of skins was counted and entered in a ledger together with Father's name. I watched carefully as a shortsighted woman with thick-lensed spectacles wrote the number of furs down in the book.

This job done, I was at a complete loss for something to do. Wait as I might, Father did not come out. So I set off, shoes in hand, and accompanied by the sound of my bare feet sticking to the corridor floor, in search of my only acquaintance in the town, the man who often came to the village with messages. He had an artificial leg, and the village, adults and children alike, referred to him as "the Clerk," though when we had medical examinations at school he also acted as a kind of assistant to the doctor.

"Hullo, Frog! You here?" he cried, getting up from his chair beyond the partition. I was a trifle indignant, but I went up to the Clerk's desk. Since the village children called him "Clerk," we could scarcely complain if he called us "Frogs." I was glad to have found him.

"So you've caught a Negro, have you, Frog?" He rattled his false leg beneath the desk.

"Mm," I said, placing the palms of my hands on the

Clerk's desk. On it stood his lunch, wrapped in yellow-stained newspaper.

"Quite a feat, uh?" he said.

Gazing at the Clerk's pallid lips, I nodded majestically, but though I wanted to tell him about the Negro, I could find no words to explain the great black man who had been brought to our village at dusk.

"The nigger—will they kill him?" I asked.

"No idea," he replied, jerking his chin in the direction of the mayor's office. "I expect they'll decide that now."

"I wonder if they'll bring him to the town," I said.

"You seem pleased to have a holiday from school," he said, evading the crucial question. "That woman teacher, she's a lazy bitch, does nothing but complain but makes no move to go. Says the village children are dirty and smell. . . ."

I felt a spasm of shame at the dirt encrusted round my neck, but I shook my head and laughed defiantly. The Clerk's false leg protruded, artificial and twisted, from beneath the desk. I liked to see him when he came hopping along the mountain road on his good leg, his false leg, and a single crutch, but when he sat in a chair his leg was unpleasant and insidious, like the town children.

Emerging from the mayor's office, my father called me in a low voice. The Clerk clapped me on the shoulder, so I clapped him on the arm in exchange and ran out of the room.

"Don't let the prisoner escape, Frog," he called after me.

"What have you decided to do with him?" I asked Father as we went back through the town in the blazing sunlight.

"Trying to get out of it all the time, the bastards," he replied vehemently, as if it were my fault. Squashed by this display of bad temper, I lapsed into silence and we walked on through the shade of the stunted, ugly trees that lined the town street. Even the trees of the town were insidious and unfriendly like its children.

When we got to the bridge on the outskirts of town,

Father seated himself on the low railing and opened his lunch-packet in silence. Still striving to stop myself asking questions, I stretched out a somewhat grubby finger to the packet on Father's lap. We ate our riceballs without exchanging a word.

At last, with stiff calves and the skin of our faces heavy with grease, sweat and grime, we left the path along the ridge of the hills and went down through the cryptomeria woods to the entrance to the village. Already twilight covered the whole valley, but the heat of the sun still lingered in our bodies, and we were grateful for the thick mist that came blowing up.

Leaving my father, who went off to report to the village head's house, I went up to the second floor of the storehouse. My brother was sitting on the bed, fast asleep. I stretched out an arm and shook him, conscious of the frailty of the bone in the shoulder bare beneath my hand. The skin under my warm palm shrank slightly, and tiredness and fear ebbed away from his suddenly-opened eyes.

"How's he been?" I asked.

"Just sleeping in the cellar," replied my brother.

"Were you scared, all by yourself?" I asked gently. He shook his head with serious eyes.

"Has Harelip seen him?" I asked.

"They shout at any children that go near the cellar," he said regretfully. "Are they coming to fetch him from town?"

"I don't know," I said.

Father and the woman from the grocer's came in downstairs, talking in loud voices. It was impossible, the woman was insisting, for her to take the Negro's food down to the cellar for him. She couldn't, she was a woman; why didn't Father get his son to do it? I was bending down to take off my shoes, but I straightened myself up. My young brother's soft hand was pressed firmly against my back. Chewing my lip, I waited for Father's voice. As soon as I heard him shout—"Hey, come down here"—I flung my shoes under the bed and ran down the stairs.

The butt end of the gun clasped against his chest, Father motioned to the basket of food the woman from the grocer's had left. I nodded in reply, and picked it up in a firm grasp. In silence we went out of the storehouse and walked through the chilly, misty outside air. The cobbles beneath the soles of our feet still held some of the warmth of the day. At the side of the storehouse, there was no grown-up standing on guard. A pale light was seeping through the skylight of the cellar; when I saw it, I felt the tiredness break out all over my body like a poison. Yet I was so excited at my first chance of seeing the Negro at close quarters that my teeth were chattering.

Father unfastened the trapdoor's ponderous padlock that distilled drops of water, then peered inside and began to climb cautiously down with his gun at the ready. I squatted waiting, the night air with its mixture of mist drops clinging insistently about my neck. My sturdy brown legs shook, shaming me before the innumerable eyes that I could feel watching me behind my back.

"Hey," Father called in a smothered voice.

I went down the short flight of stairs clasping the basket to my chest.

There, picked out in the light of a low-powered electric bulb, crouched the Negro. My gaze was drawn irresistibly to the thick chain of the boar trap that linked his black leg to a pillar. His knees were clasped to his chin, from which position he looked up at us with bloodshot eyes, with a gaze that was insistent and challenging. All the blood in my body, it seemed, came gushing into my ears and beat in crimson waves through my face. I averted my eyes and looked up at father, who leaned with his back against the wall, his gun trained on the Negro airman. He motioned at me with his chin. I went forward, almost shutting my eyes, and placed the basket of food before the Negro. As I withdrew, my guts writhed in a sudden spasm of fear, and I had to fight down a wave of nausea. The Negro airman stared, my father stared, I stared at the basket of food. A dog barked in the distance. The village square beyond the skylight was hushed in silence.

Suddenly, I felt my interest drawn to the food basket beneath the Negro's gaze. I was seeing it now with his starving eyes. A few large balls of rice, dried fish with all the fat toasted out of it, a mess of vegetables, and goat's milk in a wide-necked cut glass bottle. For a long while, until my own empty stomach began to complain, he stared at the basket of food from the same position as when I had first entered. The Negro would certainly despise the poor dinner we were offering, I thought, and would despise us, too, and would refuse to touch the food at all. A feeling of shame assailed me. If the Negro continued to show no desire to start the meal, my shame would infect Father. Father, overwhelmed by his grown-up's shame, would be driven to frenzy, and soon the village would be filled with the violence of grown-ups, faces blanched with shame. Whoever could have had the foolish notion of giving the Negro food?

But, all at once, the Negro stretched out an unbelievably long arm. With thick dark fingers that sprouted bristles along the back, he took up the bottle and, drawing it to him, smelled it. Then the bottle was tilted, the Negro's thick, rubbery lips opened to expose great pearly teeth in two orderly rows like parts inside some machine, and I watched the milk being poured into the Negro's vast, pinkly gleaming mouth. A noise came from his gullet like an air pocket in water running down a drain, and the milk overflowed the corners of his lips, lips that were almost painfully swollen, like a ripe fruit bound round with a cord. It ran down his bare throat, wetting his open shirt, and down his chest, where it formed shivering globules like oil on the tough, blackly gleaming skin. With lips dry from excitement, I realized for the first time that goat's milk was an extremely beautiful liquid.

With a loud clatter, the Negro returned the bottle to the basket. Henceforth, there was none of the original

hesitation in his movements. The rice-balls, cupped in his vast palms, looked like tiny candies. The dried fish was crunched to pieces, head-bones and all, between his glistening teeth. Leaning by Father's side against the wall, I watched with a sense of wonder the Negro airman's powerful jaws at work. He was too absorbed in his meal to pay any attention to us, so that as I struggled to quell my own hunger I had the leisure, albeit a rather choking kind of leisure, to study this magnificent catch that Father and the other grown-ups had made.

The short, crinkly hair that covered the Negro's well-shaped head formed small, tight curls rising like sooty flames above ears pricked like a wolf's. The skin at his throat and chest seemed to enfold within it a dark, grape-colored glow. His thick, greasy neck fascinated me each time it twisted to form tough folds in the skin. And the odor of his body, persistent and pervasive as nausea welling up in the throat, seeping like some corrosive poison into everything about it, brought a flush to my cheeks and awoke flashes of an emotion close to madness.

With blurred, hot eyes, I watched the rapacious way he attacked his food. As I did so, the crude provisions in the basket were transformed into a ripe, rich, exotic feast. If, when I carried the basket away, there had been any fragments of food left in it, I would have seized them with fingers that trembled with secret pleasure and gulped them down. But the Negro soldier ate up every scrap, then wiped the dish that had held the gruel clean with his finger.

Father poked me in the side. With a mixture of shame and irritation, as if I had been indulging in lewd daydreams, I went up to the Negro and took the basket. Protected by the muzzle of Father's gun, I turned my back to him and made to go up the stairs. Just then, I heard a low, thick cough from the Negro. My step faltered and the flesh all over my body crept with terror.

At the top of the stairs to the second floor of the storehouse, a murky, distorting mirror swung to and fro in a depression in the pillar. As I went up, there rose into the half-light the face of a Japanese boy, a boy with twitching cheeks who chewed on pallid, bloodless lips, an utter nonentity of a boy. With arms that hung limp and heavy, my emotions battered to the point of tears, I opened the door—unexpectedly shut—of our room.

My young brother was sitting plumped on the bed; his eyes were gleaming, hot with excitement and a little dry from fear.

"It was you shut the door, wasn't it!" I said, screwing my face into a haughty expression to distract attention from my own quivering lips.

"Mm." My brother lowered his eyes in shame at his own cowardice. "What's he like, the nigger?"

An ever-mounting tiredness was enveloping me. "Oh, just smells awful, that's all," I replied.

The next morning I awoke late to hear a murmur of voices from the open space by the side of the storehouse. Neither my brother nor Father was in the room. As I thought, Father's shotgun was not in its place. Listening to the murmur outside and gazing up at the empty gunrack, I felt my chest begin to pound furiously. I sprang up from the bed and, grabbing my undershirt, ran down the stairs.

The grown-ups were gathered in a group, and the children were among them, peering up at them with small, grubby faces petrified with apprehension.

Some distance apart from the rest, my brother and Harelip were crouching down beside the cellar skylight. "They've been looking in!" I thought with anger, and was about to run towards them when I saw the Clerk, leaning lightly on his crutch, emerge with bowed head from the cellar. An intense, dark feeling of prostration, a wave of despair, seeped throughout my body. What came next, however, was not the expected procession bearing the Negro airman's body, but my father, who emerged talking in a low voice to the village head, the gun on his shoulder still encased in its bag. I heaved a deep sigh, and the sweat poured from my armpits and crotch.

"Come and have a look!" Harelip shouted to me as I stood there. "Look!"

I lay on my belly on the hot stones and peered in through the narrow skylight just above the ground. At the bottom of the black depths, the Negro airman lay struck down on the floor, his body bent and limp like that of a domestic animal beaten into submission. I raised myself on my hands.

"Did they hit him?" I asked Harelip in a voice shaking with rage. "Did they hit him with his legs chained so he couldn't move?"

"Not them!" said Harelip regretfully. They went in and had a look at him. Just looked at him, and that's what it did to the nigger."

My rage evaporated. I shook my head noncommittally. My young brother was staring at me. "It's all right," I told him.

One of the village children who had tried to squeeze round me to peer through the skylight was kicked in the side by Harelip and raised a wail. Harelip had already taken to himself the right to peer at the Negro through the skylight, and was on tenterhooks lest anyone should violate that right.

I left Harelip and the others and went to where the Clerk was talking to the grown-ups who surrounded him. He went on talking, damaging my self-respect and the warmth I felt towards him by ignoring me just as completely as he ignored the ordinary village children with the snot dried on their upper lips. But there are times when one cannot bother about pride or self-respect; I thrust my head between the grown-ups' legs and listened to what the Clerk and the village head were saying.

At the town office and the town police station—the Clerk was saying—it was impossible for them to do anything about the disposal of the Negro prisoner. They would report the matter to the prefectural office, but until a reply came he would have to be taken care of, and the responsibility for this rested with the village. The village headman objected to this, and pointed out again and again that the village was not equipped to accommodate a Negro soldier as a prisoner. It would be difficult, too, for the villagers to provide a sufficient escort for a dangerous Negro along such a long mountain road. The long rainy season and the floods had made everything complicated and difficult.

But the Clerk had only to adopt a peremptory tone, the pompous tone of the minor bureaucrat, for the village grown-ups to give in feebly. As soon as it become clear that the Negro was to be kept in the village till the prefecture decided on its policy, I left the group of adults, their faces stiff with discontent and embarrassment, and ran to where my young brother and Harelip were sitting monopolizing the skylight. I was full of relief, and expectation, and a creeping uneasiness with which the grown-ups had infected me.

"Well, they're not killing him are they?" said Harelip triumphantly. "A nigger's not an enemy, just as I said!"

"He's too good to kill," said my brother.

And I and Harelip and my brother, foreheads pressed together, peered through the skylight and sighed with satisfaction at the sight of the Negro still sprawled limply on the floor, his chest heaving as he breathed. There were murmurs of discontent from the other children, who had come right up to where we stretched our legs along the ground with the soles of the feet turned up to dry in the sun. Harelip promptly raised himself and yelled at them, and they fled with cries of dismay.

Eventually, we grew tired of watching the Negro do nothing but lie sprawled in the same place, but we did not abandon our privileged position. Instead, Harelip allowed the other children to peep through the skylight for brief intervals, exacting from each of them some payment—in jujubes or in apricots, figs, or persimmons. They would peer in, red to the backs of their necks with surprise and excitement, then stand up rubbing the dust off their chins with the palms of their hands. As I stood with my back to the storehouse wall, watching the children baking their little buttocks in the sun, so intent, despite Harelip's harrying, on the first big experience of their lives, I felt a strange satisfaction and fullness, a blithe upsurge of excitement. One of the hunting dogs had detached itself from the group of adults and come over to us. Harelip put it over his bare knees to search for fleas, which he cracked with yellowish nails as he delivered orders, mingled with lofty imprecations, at the children.

Even after the grown-ups had gone up to the path along the ridge to see the Clerk off, we still continued our strange sport. Sometimes, ignoring the resentful voices behind our backs, we would ourselves peer long and intently into the cellar. Still the Negro airman sprawled there with no sign of motion, as if the mere gaze of the grown-ups had somehow injured him.

That night, accompanied by Father with his gun and carrying a heavy iron pot containing a coarse stew of rice and vegetables, I went down to the cellar once more. The Negro peered at us from eyes thickly crusted at the edges with yellow discharge, then thrust his hairy fingers into the hot food without further ado and began eating enthusiastically. I was able to watch at my leisure, while Father leaned against the wall looking bored, without training his gun on the Negro as before. Looking down at the slight tremors of the thick sinews in the Negro's neck, at the sudden tightening and relaxation of the muscles, I began to feel that he was docile and quiet, like some gentle animal. I looked up at Harelip and my brother, who were gazing in with bated breath, and darted a swift, crafty smile at their dusky, mistily gleaming eyes. I had begun to get used to the Negro; the fact sowed and nurtured in me the seeds of an intensely pleasurable pride. Yet every time the Negro's movements tilted the boar trap and the chain gave out a hard, metallic noise, the original terror revived in me in one mighty rush, and poured throughout my veins till I felt the skin all over my body covered with goose pimples.

From the next day, I took upon myself the privilege of carrying the Negro soldier his food, once every morning and night. Each time I was accompanied by Father, who already omitted to take the gun from his shoulder and train it on the Negro. Early in the morning and at the time between evening and night, when I appeared with Father at the side of the storehouse carrying the basket of food, a great sigh that spread and rose up into the sky like a cloud would rise from the children who had been waiting eagerly in the open space. Knitting my brows, I crossed the open space without so much as a glance at the children, in the manner of the expert who, though he has lost interest in his own work, still shows the same meticulous care in the actual performance. My young brother and Harelip had to be content to walk with me, one close at each side, as far as the cellar entrance. As soon as Father and I had gone down, they would race back to peer in through the skylight. Even if I had grown tired of the task of carrying the Negro's food, I would have continued solely for the pleasure of the fervent sighs of envy—resentment, almost—that the children, Harelip included, directed at my back as I walked.

I got my Father, however, to give special permission to Harelip to come into the cellar once every afternoon to help me with a task that was too heavy for me alone. In the cellar, a small, old tub had been placed in the shadow of a post for the Negro's use. Every afternoon, Harelip and I would go up the stair carrying it carefully, one on each side, by a thick rope passed through its handles, and would go to the village manure heap to dispose of the thick, evil-smelling liquid that made a slopping noise as we walked. Harelip showed an excessive enthusiasm for the task; sometimes, before transferring it to the big tank by the manure heap, he would stir it with a piece of wood, and explain the state of the Negro's digestion, especially his diarrhea, which he asserted was caused by the grains of corn in the rice-gruel.

Sometimes when we went, accompanied by my father, to get the tub, we would find the Negro with his trousers down, straddling the small tub with his shiny black buttocks thrust out like a mating dog. At such times, we would be kept waiting awhile behind the Negro's buttocks, and Harelip, overcome with awe and wonder, his eyes ecstatic, would hold on tightly to my arm as we listened to the furtive noise set up by the boar trap linking the Negro's legs on each side of the tub.

We children came to occupy ourselves exclusively with the Negro, who filled every corner of our lives, spreading among us like an epidemic. But adults have their work; adults are immune to the epidemics of children. The adults could not sit doing nothing until the belated directive came from the town office. When even my father—who had taken on the task of guarding the Negro—began to go out hunting, the Negro was left to exist in the cellar, solely for the purpose of fulfilling the children's daily needs.

During the daytime, I and my brother and Harelip acquired the habit of shutting ourselves up in the cellar where the Negro sat. At first, we did so with the entrancing throbbing of the breast that always accompanies the breaking of regulations. Soon, though, we got used to it and became complacent, as if to keep watch on the Negro was a sacred task entrusted to us while the adults were away in the hills and the valley. The skylight peephole, abandoned by my brother and Harelip, was handed on to the village children. Flat on their bellies on the hot, dusty ground, they would take turns peering enviously at the scene as we three sat round the Negro. Occasionally a child, forgetting himself with envy, would try to follow us into the cellar, only to be punched by Harelip for his mutiny and to fall to the ground with a bloody nose.

By now, we would carry the Negro's bucket only as far as the top of the cellar steps. The smelly task of carrying it to the communal manure heap under the blazing sun we entrusted to the children we deigned to appoint to the task. The designated children, their cheeks glowing with pleasure, would keep it perfectly upright as they carried it there, careful not to spill a single drop of the muddy, yellowish liquid that seemed so precious to them. And every morning all the children, ourselves included, would look up at the path that came down through the wood from the road along the ridge, almost praying that the Clerk would not come down it bearing the dreaded order.

The Negro's ankle where the boar trap was fastened was raw and inflamed, and the blood from it stuck shrunken on his instep like dried blades of grass. The damaged skin with its pink sore was a constant worry to us. When he straddled the tub, the Negro would bare his teeth like a grinning child in the effort to withstand the pain. After long searching of each other's eyes and long consultations, we determined to remove the trap from his ankles. After all, he did nothing but sit in silence in the cellar, hands clasped round his knees, his eyes veiled with some thick liquid that might be either tears or discharge—just like some black, dull-witted animal, in fact. What harm could he possibly do us? He was only a nigger, after all.

Clasping the key I had fetched out of Father's toolbox, Harelip bent down, almost touching the Negro's knee with his shoulder, and removed the trap. At once, with something like a moan, the Negro stood up and shook his legs. Harelip flung the trap at the wall and fled up the stairs shedding tears of fright; my brother and I merely clung to each other, unable even to stand up, paralyzed by a rewakened fear of the Negro. But he did not pounce on us like a hawk: instead, he sat down again with his knees clasped in his hands, and fixed his eyes, damp and bleary with tears and discharge, on the trap where it had fallen by the wall. When Harelip, bowed with shame, came back to the cellar, my brother and I greeted him with gentle smiles. The Negro was as well-behaved as any domestic animal....

Late that night, when Father came to fasten the great padlock on the cellar trapdoor, he looked at the soldier's freed ankles. I was suffocating with apprehension, but he did not scold me as expected. The Negro was as gentle as a tame animal—by now the idea had seeped into the minds of all the villagers, children and adults alike.

The next morning when I and my brother and Harelip went to give him his breakfast, we found the Negro fumbling with the boar trap, which he held on his lap. The part where the trap shut together had been broken when Harelip had thrown it against the wall, and the Negro was examining the broken part with the same sure, expert touch as the trap-mender who came to the village every spring. Suddenly, he raised his shining black forehead to gaze at me and indicated by means of gestures what it was he wanted. I and Harelip looked at each other, unable to suppress the delight that smoothed the tension from our cheeks. The Negro was talking to us, he was talking to us just like the animals talked to us....

We ran to the village head's house and brought out on our shoulders the toolbox, one of the village's communal pieces of property, and carried it to the cellar. Though it contained things that might serve as weapons, we did not hesitate to entrust it to the Negro soldier. For us, the idea that this Negro, so like a domestic animal, had once been a fighting soldier was incredible. It defied all imagination.

The Negro stared first at the toolbox, then into our eyes. We watched him, our bodies thrilling with pleasure, and when Harelip said to me in a low voice, "He's just like a human!" I poked my young brother in the buttocks and laughed myself almost sick, so happy and proud I felt. Through the skylight, a sigh of wonder wafted in like a gust of mist from the children outside.

We took back the breakfast basket and ate our own breakfast. When we came back to the cellar the Negro had got a wrench and a small hammer out of the toolbox and had set them out in orderly fashion on a sack spread on the floor. He looked at us as we went and sat by him.

Suddenly, his great, rapidly yellowing teeth bared, and his cheeks relaxed into folds; with something like a shock we learned for the first time that the Negro soldier laughed. And we found that we were bound to him by a deep, fierce, almost "human" bond.

Late afternoon came. Harelip was taken home, amidst much foul abuse, by the woman from the blacksmith's, and our buttocks began to hurt where they rested directly on the bare floor—yet still the Negro went on, trying to make the part where the trap sprang together fit properly. His fingers were dirty with the ancient, dust-laden grease from the trap, and he set up a soft, metallic noise as he worked.

I watched untiringly the way the soft, pink flesh of his palms yielded under the pressure of the blade of the trap, and the way the greasy dirt on his neck twisted together to form a dark line as he moved. It awoke in me a not unpleasant nausea, a faint revulsion that was somehow linked with desire. The Negro was intent on his work, puffing out the thick flesh of his cheeks as if he were singing softly to himself within his capacious mouth. My brother leaned against my knee, watching the movements of his fingers with eyes that shone with admiration. A swarm of flies flew about us, reverberating and persistent, the sound of their wings tangled with the heat deep in our ears.

With a sound that grew more and more intense, shorter and more incisive, the trap bit into the rough straw rope placed between it, until finally the Negro laid it carefully on the floor and looked at us with smiling, dull-witted, liquid eyes. The sweat was running in trembling jewels down his black, gleaming forehead. My brother and I smiled back at him. Still smiling, we gazed at length into his gentle eyes, just as we did with the goats or the hounds. It was hot. We smiled at each other, soaked through and through in the heat, as though the heat were a pleasure we and the Negro shared, binding us together.

One morning the Clerk was brought in all muddy and bleeding from his chin. He had fallen in the woods, tumbled down a short bank and stayed there helpless till the village grown-ups, finding him there on their way to work in the hills, had helped him up again. The part where the hard, thick leather of his false leg was attached by a metal ring had bent, and it refused to fit on properly. The Clerk stared at it perplexedly while the village headman was giving him treatment. He made no move to pass on any directive from the town. The grown-ups grew irritable, while we children reflected that, if he had come to get the Negro soldier, he would have done better to starve to death at the bottom of the bank. In fact, though, he had come to explain that still no directive had come from the prefectural authorities. We promptly recovered our happiness and good spirits, and with them our goodwill toward the Clerk. We took his false leg and the toolbox down to the cellar.

The Negro was sprawled on the clammy cellar floor singing in a deep, rich voice, singing a strangely vivid song that fascinated us, a song in which both grief and triumph crouched ready to spring on us at any moment. We showed him the broken false leg. He got up, stared at it for a moment, then set to work without more ado. A cry of delight sprang through the skylight from the children peering in. Harelip, my brother and I laughed till we gasped for breath.

By evening, when the Clerk came into the cellar, the false leg was as good as new. He fastened it on his short stump and stood up, to a second cry of joy from the children. He hopped up the stairs and went out into the open space to see how his leg worked. Dragging the Negro by both arms, we pulled him to his feet and without the slightest hesitation, as though it were a longstanding habit, took him out with us.

His broad nostrils distended to breathe in to the full, fresh air of the summer evening—the first air above ground he had breathed since becoming a prisoner. Eagerly, he watched the Clerk's trial steps. Everything was perfect. The Clerk came back running, and took from his pocket one of the cigarettes he made himself from knotweed leaves.

They were crudely made, with smoke that smarted when it got into your eyes and reminded you of a forest fire. He lit it and handed it to the tall Negro. The Negro took one drag at it and doubled up, coughing desperately with his hand clasped to his throat. The Clerk, embarrassed, gave a mournful kind of smile, but we children roared with laughter. The Negro straightened up, wiped away the tears with his great hand, then drew from the linen trousers that tightly encased his muscular hindquarters a black, shining pipe, and held it out to the Clerk. The Clerk accepted the gift, the Negro nodded contentedly, and a shaft of sunlight poured down, casting on them the purple shadows of evening. We crowded round them, shouting till our throats hurt and laughing crazily.

In the end, we would often invite the Negro soldier out of his cellar to walk with us along the cobbled road through the village, and the grown-ups made no complaint. Just as they would step aside into the undergrowth out of the way of the village bull that lived at the village headman's house, so they would step to one side with averted faces whenever they met the Negro soldier walking along the road surrounded by us children.

Even when the children were conscripted for work in their houses and were too busy to visit the Negro in his cellar home, he would come up to the open space by the storehouse and doze in the shade of the trees, or walk slowly, with rounded shoulders, along the village road. Children and grown-ups alike, we would notice him without any feeling of astonishment. He was already becoming a component of village life, in the same way as the hunting dogs, or the children, or the trees.

Sometimes, Father would come home at dawn carrying at his side a long, narrow trap, rudely made of nailed boards, in which a weasel with a plump, improbably long body would be raging about. On these days, I and my brother would have to spend the whole morning on the bare floor of the storehouse, helping with the skinning, and we would pray that the Negro would come and watch us at work.

Whenever he came, we would kneel with bated breath on either side of Father as he grasped the bloodstained skinning knife by its greasy handle; and we would hope for the sake of our spectator, the Negro, that the death of the rebellious, agile weasel would be satisfactory and its skining skillful. As it was strangled it would release a fearsome stink, a last gesture of spite out of its death-throes. A slight splitting noise as its skin was sliced open by the dully gleaming tip of Father's knife, and finally its body would lie before us wrapped in flesh of a pearly luster, small and obscene in its nakedness. By the time we had carried its insides to the manure heap, taking care not to spill them, thrown them away, and come back wiping our hands on large tree leaves, the weasel skin was already being nailed inside out to the wall, the fatty layer and the fine blood-vessels gleaming in the sun. Pursing his lips and emitting a whistling noise, the Negro would gaze at the creases that formed in the skin as Father scraped off the fat with his thick fingertips so that it would dry quickly. And when, at last, he saw the fur spread out on the wall, dried hard as a fingernail, with the blood-colored marks running over it like railways on a map, he would marvel at it till my brother and I were overcome with pride at Father's skill. Even Father would sometimes pause in his task of spraying water on the pelts to give a friendly glance at the Negro soldier. At such times, I and my brother and the Negro and Father would be bound together as if we were one family centered around Father's skill with the weasels.

He also liked to peer in at the blacksmith's workshop. Sometimes, particularly when Harelip was helping the smith make hoes, the bare upper half of his body gleaming in the light of the fire, we children would go to the blacksmith's hut with the Negro in our midst. When the blacksmith picked up a red-hot lump of iron with his charcoal-begrimed fingers and thrust it into water, the Negro would cry out with wonder, while the children applauded. The blacksmith himself grew proud, and would often take this dangerous method of displaying his prowess.

Even the women lost their fear of the Negro, and would sometimes give him food directly from their own hands.

Summer reached its height, and still no directive came from the prefectural government. There were rumors that the town where the prefectural offices stood had been ruined in an air raid, but these rumors had no effect on us. Hotter than any fire that might burn the town was the air that, day after day, enshrouded our village. About the Negro's person as we sat with him in the still, unventilated cellar, there began to press a dense, greasy, almost overpowering smell, a smell that reminded one of the rotting weasel flesh on the village manure heap. It was a constant source of amusement to us, and we would laugh about it till the tears came; but when his skin began to get sweaty it stank so that we were unable to stay near him.

One hot afternoon, Harelip proposed that we take the Negro airman to the spring that formed the village's communal source of water. Disgusted with ourselves for not thinking of it before, we grasped him by his filthy, sticky hands and pulled him up the stairs. The children gathered in the open space outside surrounded us with shouts, and we ran off along the road that lay burning in the sun.

We stripped naked as plucked fowls, peeled off the Negro's clothes, and jumped in a crowd into the very center of the spring, where we splashed water at each other and set up a great clamor, entranced at our latest idea. The naked Negro was so large that even at the deepest part of the spring the water only just came up to his waist. Every time we threw water at him, he would shriek like a strangled hen and thrust his head below the surface. There he would remain till he was forced to stand up again, shouting and spouting water at the same time. His naked, wet body, reflecting the strong rays of the sun, shone like the body of a black horse; it was perfect, and beautiful. Suddenly, we noticed that the Negro had a splendid, a heroic, an unbelievably beautiful phallus. We gathered around him clamoring, bumping our naked bodies against each other, and when he grasped it and, taking up a fierce, threatening stance, gave a great bellow, we dashed water on him and laughed till the tears ran down our cheeks.

We looked on him as on some rare, wonderful domestic animal, a genius of an animal. What words now can express the love we felt for the Negro airman, or the richness and rhythm of the sunlight glittering on his wet, heavy skin on that far-off, bright summer afternoon; of the deep shadows on the cobbles; of the smell of the children's and the Negro's bodies; of the voices hoarse with delight?

To us, it began to seem that this summer of bared, gleaming muscles—this summer that like a suddenly-gushing oil well sprayed, covered us, with a thick black oil of delight —would go on forever without end: could never end.

On the evening of the day of our old-style ablutions, a thunderstorm wrapped the valley in mist, and rain fell throughout the night. The next morning, as I and my brother and Harelip took the Negro his food, we had to cling to the wall of the storehouse to avoid the unceasing downpour. After the meal, he sat in the dark cellar with his hands clasped about his knees, singing in a low voice. We stood, spreading our fingers out to catch the spray of the rain that splashed in through the skylight, washed by the swell of the Negro's voice as he sang, by the songs weighty and solemn as the sea.

By the time he had finished his singing, the rain had stopped spraying through the skylight. Tugging at his arm, we took him, still smiling, out into the village square. The mist had suddenly cleared from the valley, and the trees were fat and swollen like young pullets with the raindrops they had absorbed into their dense foliage. At each slight breeze, they shook daintily, scattering wet leaves and raindrops to form momentary rainbows into which the cicadas started. We sat on the stone slab at the entrance to the cellar, breathing in the scent of the wet trees amidst the reviving heat of the day and a storm of cicada voices.

We were still in the same position when, past noon, the Clerk, his umbrella under his arm, came down the path through the woods and went to the village head's house. We stood up and leaned against the dripping old apricot tree, waiting for the Clerk to come hopping out of the shadowy depths of the house so that we could wave a signal to him. But wait as we might, he did not emerge again. Instead, the alarm bell on the building near the village head's house rang out to summon back the adults from the valley and woods where they were working, and the women and children of the village emerged into the road from the rain-sodden houses.

Turning round to the Negro, I saw that the smile had gone from his brown-lustered face, and my chest constricted with a sudden uneasiness. Leaving the Negro behind, I and my brother and Harelip ran to the entrance of the village headman's house.

The Clerk, who was standing silent in the entrance, ignored us. The village headman, who was sitting cross-legged on the raised, boarded portion of the floor, was sunk in thought. Impatiently, struggling to check hopes we felt would be disappointed, we waited for the grown-ups to assemble. Gradually, they came back from the fields and woods, still in their working clothes, their cheeks puffed out discontentedly. Father came in too, with several small birds fastened to the barrel of his gun.

No sooner had the conference begun than the Clerk dashed the children's hopes by explaining, in the local dialect, that it had been decided the Negro airman should be handed over to the prefectural authorities. Properly speaking, he said, the army ought to come and get him, but the army was apparently in confusion and at loggerheads with itself, so they had asked the village people to take him as far as the town. For the grown-ups, the only inconvenience was the task of turning in the Negro, but we children were in the depths of alarm and despondency. If they handed over the Negro, what would be left in the village afterwards? Nothing but the empty shell of a summer....

I had to give the Negro warning. I squeezed my way out between the grown-ups' legs and ran back to where he was still sitting in the open space before the storehouse. As I stopped before him, gasping for breath, he slowly turned his great, lackluster eyes up to look at me. I, who could convey nothing to him, could only gaze at him with a mixture of sadness and frustration. His arms about his knees, he gazed searchingly into my eyes. His lips, rounded like the belly of some pregnant freshwater fish, hung loosely open, and the saliva trickled white and gleaming between his teeth. I turned and saw the grown-ups, led by the Clerk, emerge from the dark entrance of the village head's house and come towards the storehouse.

I shook the seated Negro by the shoulder and called to him in the local dialect. I was almost faint with frustration. What could I do? Silent, he let himself be shaken by my arm, his great head rolling from side to side. Drooping my head, I let go his shoulder.

Then suddenly, he rose to his feet and towered before me like a tree. Grasping my upper arm, he dragged me to him and, pressing me tightly to his body, ran down the cellar steps. Dumbfounded, for awhile I could only watch idly the movements of his firm thighs and the contractions of the flesh on his buttocks as he went swiftly about the cellar. He lowered the trapdoor, then, taking the boar trap that still hung there as he had mended it, chained together the ring intended for the bolt on the inside of the trapdoor and the trapdoor support that projected from the wall. Hands clasped together, head bowed, he came down the stairs again. As I looked into his expressionless eyes, the realization swept in on me that the Negro soldier had changed back into the black wild beast that defied understanding, the dangerously poisonous substance that he had been when he was first brought back captive. I looked up at his great form, then across at the boar trap fastening the trapdoor, then down at my own small, bare feet. Fear and shock flooded and whirled through my guts. I sprang away from the Negro and pressed my back against the wall, but he remained in the middle of the cellar, head bowed.

I bit at my lip in the effort to quell the trembling of my lower limbs.

The grown-ups came to the top of the trapdoor and began to shake the boar trap fastened to it—gently at first, then with the frenzy of a fowl that has suddenly been attacked. But the thick oak lid, the lid that had once been so reassuring to the grown-ups when they had used it to shut the Negro airman in the cellar, was now shutting them all outside—the village grown-ups, and the children, and the trees, and the valley.

Through the skylight peered in panic-stricken grown-up faces, promptly to be replaced, with a clumsy bumping of foreheads, by others, A sudden change in the approach of the grown-ups outside was apparent. At first, they had shouted. Now they fell silent, and the menacing barrel of a gun was thrust through the skylight. Like a nimble animal, the Negro leapt at me and clasped me tightly to his body to protect himself from the muzzle. Groaning with the pain and wriggling in the Negro's arms, I realized the cruel truth: I was a captive, and a hostage. The Negro had been transformed into the "enemy," while my own side were clamoring beyond the trapdoor. Rage and humiliation, and the frustrating sorrow of betrayal, ran through my body, scorching it like fire. Worst of all, fear swelled up in a vortex within me, threatening to choke me.

Caught in the Negro's rough arms, I burned with rage and wept at the same time. The Negro soldier had taken me prisoner....

The gun barrel was withdrawn, the clamor from the grown-ups became louder, then a long conference started on the other side of the skylight. The Negro, still gripping my arm so tightly it was numbed by the pain, retired into a corner where there was no fear of sniping and sat down in silence. I was dragged towards him till, just as I had done when we were friends, I knelt bare-kneed by him, surrounded by the close, oppressive odor of his body. The grown-ups talked for a long while. From time to time, my father peered in through the skylight. Each time he nodded to his hostage son, I wept.

The tide of evening came in, first to the cellar, then to the open space beyond the skylight. As darkness fell, the adults went off home a few at a time, casting words of encouragement to me as they went. For long after, I heard Father's footsteps walking on the other side of the skylight, but suddenly the last trace of humanity disappeared from the earth above, and night filled the cellar.

The Negro released my arm, and gazed at me as if suddenly gripped by the friendly, everyday feeling that had welled between us till that morning. Shaking with anger, I averted my eyes and stayed with head down, shoulders obstinately hunched, till he turned his back on me and squatted with his head between his knees. I was alone. Like a weasel caught in a weasel trap, I was forlorn, solitary, utterly despairing. The Negro soldier was motionless in the gloom.

I stood up, went to the stairs and touched the boar trap, but it was cold and hard, repelling my fingers and the unformed buds of hope they harbored. I was like the baby hare that weakens and dies still staring at the iron scissors clasping its wounded leg, unable to believe the depths into which it has fallen or the trap that has caught it. I was tortured by my foolishness in trusting the Negro as a friend. And yet, could anyone have doubted that great, smelly, ever-smiling black man?

A cold shivering gripped me and my teeth chattered. My belly had begun to hurt. I squatted down with my hands pressed against the lower part of it, and was struck by an acutely embarrassing realization: I was going to have diarrhea. The raw state of the nerves all over my body was only helping to bring it on. Yet I could do nothing about it in front of the Negro. I fought against it, clenching my teeth, the hard-wrung sweat dabbling my forehead. I fought against it, suffering, till the effort of fighting it overcame even my fear.

In the end, however, I gave in. I went to the tub—the

tub that had made us so hilarious when the Negro had straddled it—and lowered my trousers. To me, my white, stripped buttocks seemed infinitely weak and defenseless: shame, it seemed, would dye everything black inside me, from my throat, down my gullet and right to the lining of my stomach. Finally, I stood up again and went back to the corner. I was broken, abject, in the deepest depths of degradation. I pressed my grubby forehead against the wall—I could feel the warmth of the soil through it—and cried unceasingly in a low voice. The night was long. In the woods, a pack of wild dogs barked. The air had grown cold. Tiredness took heavy possession of me, and I slumped to the floor and slept.

When I awoke, the Negro's palm was pressed down as before on my half-numbed arm. The breeze through the skylight brought in a swirling mist, mingled with the voices of the grown-ups. I could hear the Clerk's false leg, too, creaking as he walked about. Soon, there came amidst the other noises the noise of a heavy hammer beating at the trapdoor. The heavy, powerful sound echoed in my hungry belly, sending sharp pains through it.

The Negro gave a sudden shout and, seizing my shoulders, pulled me to my feet. Dragging me to the middle of the cellar, he held me up to the gaze of the grown-ups beyond the skylight. Of the reason for his action, I had no idea. Through the skylight, countless eyes gazed on my shame as I dangled there like a rabbit. If my young brother's moist black eyes had been among them, I would likely have bitten off my tongue with shame. But the eyes that thronged the peephole, gazing at me, were all those of grown-ups.

The noise of the hammer grew fiercer. The Negro gave a shout, and his great hands grasped my throat from behind. The nails dug painfully into the soft skin, and the pressure on my Adam's apple made it difficult to breathe. I threshed with my hands and feet, drew my head back and gave a moan. Filled with bitter shame at being seen thus by the grown-ups beyond the skylight, I twisted in an effort to escape from the Negro's body that pressed tightly against my back, and kicked his shins with my heels. But his thick, hairy arms were hard and unyielding and his shouts were louder than my moans. The faces of the grown-ups withdrew from the other side of the skylight. Probably, I thought, they had yielded to the Negro's threat and had run to stop the others breaking in the trapdoor. The Negro's cries ceased and the pressure that was like a rock at my throat slackened. My feeling of closeness to and love for the grown-ups returned.

But the beating at the trapdoor became all the fiercer. Once more grown-up faces peered in through the skylight, and with a cry the Negro tightened his grip about my throat again. Fight it down as I might, the lips in my flung-back face opened crookedly and a feeble scream, like the cry of some small animal in distress, escaped. Even the grown-ups, then, had abandoned me. They were going on with their task of smashing in the trapdoor, leaving me to be strangled by the Negro airman. When they had finally smashed it, they would find me with cold limbs, strangled to death like one of Father's weasels. I burned with hatred. In despair, I groaned aloud at the shame of it, my head flung back, and the tears flowed as I writhed and listened to the noise of the hammer.

The rushing of innumerable wheels filled my ears, reverberated, and blood from my nose ran down my cheeks. The trapdoor was smashed, there was a rush of muddy feet, feet hairy to the backs of their toes, and the cellar was filled with ugly grown-ups half crazed with anger. Yelling at the top of his voice, the Negro clasped me tightly against his body and edged back towards the wall. I felt my back and buttocks pressed closely to his sweaty, sticky body, and a burning current like a spasm of anger seemed to pass between us. I was filled with shame and naked enmity, like a cat discovered at its mating: enmity towards the grown-ups crowded motionless at the top of the steps watching my shame; enmity towards the Negro soldier whose fat hands were pressed around my throat, their nails biting into the soft skin, staining it with blood; and a confused, irritable enmity towards anything and everything. The Negro was baying like a dog. The sound paralyzed my eardrums, and I felt myself, there in the cellar at the height of summer, sinking gradually into a profound, satisfying insensibility that was close to pleasure. The Negro's fierce breath covered the back of my neck.

From the cluster of grown-ups my father stepped forward, a hatchet in his hand. His eyes were ablaze with anger, hot like those of a dog. The Negro's nails bit deeper into my neck, and I moaned. Father rushed at us brandishing the hatcher above his head. I shut my eyes. Grasping my left wrist, the Negro pulled my arm up to protect his head. A howl rose from the crowd assembled in the cellar, and I heard the smashing of my left hand and the Negro's skull. On the oily, shiny skin of the Negro's arm beneath my chin the blood splashed down in thick globules. The grown-ups rushed towards us, and simultaneously I felt the slackening of the Negro's arm and a burning pain throughout my body.

Gradually, within a sticky, clinging bag, my hot eyelids, burning throat and scorching hand began to knit together to give me shape once more. Yet still I could not break through the sticky membrane and escape from the bag. Like a prematurely born lamb, I was enveloped in a wrapping that clung clammily to the fingers. I could not even move my body. It was night, and the grown-ups were talking round about me. Then it was morning, and I could feel the light beyond my eyelids. Sometimes a heavy palm would press against my forehead and I would moan and try to shake myself free, but my head would not move.

It was again morning when I first succeeded in opening my eyes. I was on my own bed in the storehouse. In front of the door stood Harelip and my young brother, watching me. I opened my eyes wider and moved my lips. Harelip and my brother rushed shouting down the stairs, and my father and the woman from the grocer's came up. I was famished, but as soon as Father put a feeding-cup of goat's milk to my lips I was shaken by nausea. I screamed and pressed my lips together so that drops of milk ran down my throat and neck. All grown-ups, including my father, were intolerable to me. The grown-ups, who had set on me with bared teeth, brandishing hatchets, were strange, past my understanding, and nauseating. I continued screaming until my father and the others left the room.

Time passed, and I felt my brother's soft arm quickly touch my body. Without speaking or opening my eyes, I listened to him speak in a low voice. How he had helped collect brushwood to cremate the Negro soldier; how the Clerk had brought in an order calling off the cremation. How the grown-ups had carried the body to a disused mine in the valley to prevent putrefaction, and were making a barricade to keep off the wild dogs.

He had thought I was dead. My brother kept repeating it in an awestruck voice. For two days I had done nothing but lie there without eating a thing, and he had thought I had died.

In my brother's hands I drifted off into the sleep that lured me strongly, pulled me down into it like death itself.

I woke again in the afternoon and noticed for the first time that a cloth was bound round my broken hand. I stayed perfectly still for a long time, gazing at the unrecognizably swollen arm across my chest. There was no one in the room. A disgusting smell crept in through the window. I knew what it meant, but no sadness welled up inside me.

The room grew dusky and the air chilly. I raised myself on the bed and after a long hesitation tied together the ends of the cloth around my smashed hand and looped it over my head. Then, leaning at the open window, I looked down on the village. The air above the cobbled road, above the buildings, and above the valley in which they rested was filled with the stench that welled up from the dead Negro's heavy body, and with the voiceless cry of the corpse that became ever more bloated, enveloping our bodies and spreading over our heads as in some nightmare. It was dusk. The sky, a tearful gray tinged from within with orange, lay low and constricting over the valley.

From behind the storehouse, piercing the smell of the Negro's corpse, arose a fierce clamor of children's voices. Treading carefully, with legs that shook as after a long illness, I went down the dark stairs and walked along the deserted road towards where the children were shouting.

The children were in a crowd on the grassy slope that ran down to the stream at the bottom of the valley, and their dogs were rushing about them barking. The grown-ups were at the shrub-covered bottom of the valley below the slope, still busy building a sturdy barrier to keep the dogs out of the mine where the Negro's body was kept. The dull noise of stakes being driven into the earth came up from where they were. The grown-ups were silent as they worked, but the children were rushing about shouting gleefully.

Leaning against the trunk of an old paulownia tree, I watched the children playing. They were using the tail from the Negro's aircraft as a sled for sliding down the grassy slopes. Seated astride the sharp-edged, wonderfully buoyant tail, they glided like young animals down over the grass. Whenever the sled was in danger of colliding with one of the black rocks that stuck out of the grass here and there, the boy on board would stick a bare foot into the grass and change its course. So light were the children and the sled that by the time one of them came pulling it up again, the grass he had battered down on his descent was already slowly rising again to obscure the traces of his intrepid passage. Down they would slide, shouting, the dogs barking in pursuit, and up they would come again dragging the sled behind them. An irrepressible exhilaration seemed to crackle and dart about their bodies.

Harelip detached himself from the group of children and came running towards me, chewing a stalk of grass stuck between his teeth. He leaned against the stump of an oak tree shaped like a deer's foot and peered into my face. I turned my face away from him and pretended to be absorbed in the sledding. Harelip stared fixedly at the arm that hung in a sling from my neck and sniffed noisily.

"It stinks," he said. "The hand you got smashed stinks awful, doesn't it."

I gazed back into Harelip's eyes. They glittered with the light of battle, and he took up a belligerent stance, legs apart, in readiness for an onslaught from me. But I ignored it, and instead of flying at his throat said in a hoarse, energy-less voice, "It's not me that smells. It's the smell of the nigger."

Harelip gazed at me aghast. Biting my lip, I averted my eyes from Harelip's and looked down at the tiny, narrow blades of grass that frothed over his bare ankles. He shrugged his shoulders in disdain, spat vigorously and was off, running shouting back to his fellows with the sled.

I was no longer a child.... The thought filled me like a revelation. The bloody battles with Harelip, the bird-catching on moonlit nights, the sledding, the wild dog puppies—these were all things for children. Such means of connecting oneself to the world were all remote from me now.

Exhausted, chilled and shaking, I sat down on the earth where the warmth of day still lingered. As I lowered my body, the adults, silent at their work, disappeared behind the wild, lush, summer grass, while the children suddenly reared up black against the sky like fauns.

"Hey! Your old self again, Frog?"

A dry, hot hand pressed my head from behind, but I made no move to turn and stand up. My face still turned towards the children playing on the slope, I looked out of the corner of my eye at the Clerk's black false leg planted by my bare knee. Even the Clerk's presence made my throat go dry.

"No sledding for you, Frog?" he said. "I thought it was your idea in the first place."

I was obstinately silent. Sitting down with a clatter of his false leg, the Clerk took from his jacket the pipe the

Negro had presented to him and filled it with his own tobacco. There rose from it a strong smell that irritated the soft membranes of the nostrils, a scent like a forest of many different trees on fire that enveloped the Clerk and me in the same pale blue haze.

"War's a terrible thing when it comes to this," he said. "Smashing a kid's fingers. . . ."

I took a deep breath and remained silent. The war, that vast, bloody struggle, must still be going on, the war which, like the floods that wash away flocks of sheep and close-cropped lawns in distant lands, ought never to have reached our village. Yet it had come, smashing my fingers and hand to a pulp and making my father wield a hatchet, drunk in the blood of war.

"It seems the end's not far off, when all's said and done," said the Clerk solemnly, as if talking to another grown-up. "When you try to contact the army in the town everything's in such chaos you can't get through. Don't know what to do."

The sound of the hammer still echoed from the bottom of the valley.

"They're still hard at it, aren't they," said the Clerk, pricking up his ears at the sound. "Your father and the rest of them, they don't know what to do either, that's why they're wasting time knocking in stakes."

We listened in silence to the heavy sound of the hammer that came through the lulls in the children's shouting and laughter. After awhile, the Clerk began taking off his false leg with practiced fingers. I gazed at him.

"Hey," he called out to the children. "Bring the sled to me."

The children came up with a great clamor, dragging the sled with them.

Hopping on his one leg, the Clerk pushed his way through the children surrounding the sled, while I took up the false leg and ran down the grassy slope clasping it to me. It was extremely heavy, and to hold it to me with one arm was difficult and frustrating.

The first dew was already in the lush grass; it wetted my bare feet, which itched with the blades of grass that stuck to them. I waited at the bottom of the slope, still holding the false leg in my arm. It was night already. Only the voices of the children at the top of the slope shook the film of ever-thickening, almost opaque, dark air.

A louder burst of shouting and laughter, and the soft swish of grass, but no sled came gliding down towards me, pushing its way through the sticky air. I seemed to hear a dull thud, but I stayed motionless, gazing into the twilight air. A short silence, then I saw the plane tail gliding down unoccupied towards me, twisting round as it came. I hurled the false leg from me and raced up the damp field.

By the side of an outcrop of rock that lay, damp and black with dew, bare amidst the surrounding grass, the Clerk lay staring up at the sky, his arms stretched out limply at his sides. I bent over and saw the blood that ran thick and muddy from the nostrils and ears of his smiling face. The murmur of children running down the dark field came louder against the breeze that blew up from the valley.

Afraid of being surrounded by the children, I forsook the Clerk's body and stood up in the grass. Quite quickly, I had become familiar with sudden death and with the faces of death, now sad, now smiling—just as the grown-ups in the town were familiar with them. The Clerk, I imagined, would be burned with the wood they had collected to burn the Negro....

With tear-filled eyes, I looked up at the narrow white stretch of sky where twilight still lingered, then set off down the field in search of my brother.

Translated by John Bester

Kenzaburō Ōe (pronounced "oh-eh") was born and reared in a rural community in Ehime, Shikoku, in 1935. At the age of twenty-two, while still a student of French literature at Tokyo University, he won acclaim as one of postwar Japan's most promising new writers with a short story, "Lavish Are the Dead." A year later, in 1958, he was awarded the Akutagawa Prize for "The Catch." His development as a writer has been most influenced by the works of Jean-Paul Sartre. He has written several volumes of short stories and essays, as well as a dozen major novels, two of which have been published in English: *The Silent Cry* and *A Personal Matter.* The translator of the latter work, John Nathan, has called Ōe "the most dynamic and restlessly modern writer on the Japanese literary scene."

Haruo Umezaki

Sakurajima

AT THE BEGINNING OF JULY, I was at Bōnotsu. This is where in ancient times the envoys to T'ang China used to embark. I was serving in a base signals unit, on a pass overlooking the lovely little harbor. I was one of the cipher personnel. Every day, I used to slide down the cliff and go fishing, or go into the mountains to pick myrica, or get off with the girl clerk from the Bōnotsu Post Office, who went over the pass morning and evening; any outside observer would have thought I was having a very easy time. There were very few messages—one or two a day. Some days none at all. But even while leading this kind of life, I became acutely conscious of something unseen gradually tightening its ring around me and hemming me in. I felt on edge, and grew bored with amusing myself day after day. Regularly once a day, U. S. bombers roared over the pass. Looking up at them, you could see their wings glinting ominously like knife blades as they caught the early summer sunlight.

One morning a message came. I got out the appropriate Navy code book and decoded it.

"Petty Officer Murakami posted to Sakurajima. To report immediately to H. Q. at Taniyama."

In the afternoon, my relief, Seaman First Class Tagami, arrived.

That night I had a binge all by myself on alcohol mixed

with water. Walking blind drunk along the road on the pass, I overbalanced and fell about six feet down the cliff. I cut my eyelid and lost a lot of blood. I lay on my back in a hollow, looking at the frighteningly pale moon. In my drunken state my mind was incapable of any coherent thought, and I saw myself frantically running in pursuit of some dreary phantom.

Next morning, I had some simple treatment for my eyelid at the sick bay and set out on the pass. I was to go on foot to Makurasaki. Bōnotsu, now that I was never in my life going to see it again, looked quite alarmingly clear and fresh. I turned round again and again to stare at it. "Why does it all look so alive?" I wondered, feeling a gnawing bitterness inside me. Of all the thoughts and feelings I had experienced at this base, wasn't this impression the only one that was true? Even though it was to some extent a question of sentimental feelings about parting having greatly distorted my vision....

I went by train from Makurasaki to a small town where I was to change to a bus. But there was only one bus a day, and it had already been through.

I could still have hailed a Service truck and got a lift, but I was too lazy even to do that, and went into a hotel in the center of the town. I had a meal. While I was standing on the veranda gazing at the colors in the evening sky, a young Naval officer who was passing came up and spoke to me. I told him why I was traveling. Then we went to his room and ate roasted beans and chatted for awhile.

His name was Tani, and he was a lieutenant in command of the observation unit stationed in an exposed position up on the mountain above Bōnotsu. He was short and thickset, with large eyes. He looked about twenty-three or twenty-four. He said that when Hakata had been bombed a few days before, he had been in the office of the Resident Naval Officer. He described what had happened. Hakata is where I was born, and I felt sad thinking of my friends and acquaintances living there.

"Dying a fine death, wanting to die a fine death, all that's nothing but sentimentality, don't you agree?" Lt. Tani said, looking searchingly at my face as he spat out the bean skins.

It grew dark, and I decided to stay the night. Tani suggested a little spree, so we left the hotel and made our way to a brothel behind the station. The house the hotel maid had directed us to was a dilapidated building standing on its own in a dark street, surrounded by a hedge and looking quite unlike a brothel. Along the foot of the cliff in front of the house a railway engine was going slowly by, belching red flames from its smokestack. A sudden shower of sparks was falling over the track. A thick layer of cloud seemed to hang over the starless sky.

It turned out that there was only one girl in the house. And there was no saké. At Lt. Tani's suggestion I prepared some lots. The prospect of sleeping with a woman in a place like this was dismal, and I hoped I would not win. But I did. Lt. Tani just had a cup of tea, then got up with a smile and said, "So long." After awhile, I heard the sound of his boots as he walked across the flagstones from the porch to the gate. Presently a girl came into the room. She had no right ear.

I knew that this would be the last time in my life that I would have a woman. Once I got to Sakurajima, there would be no passes out. The job waiting for me was one where you had to use any spare time there was for sleeping. I sat by the window and looked at the girl without saying a word. She made some fresh tea, trying all the time to conceal half her face from me. Suddenly a violent spasm of some unaccountable emotion akin to anger knifed through me.

I was sorely tempted to throw out some rude remark like, "I suppose it's very convenient being without an ear when you sleep on your side." This was because I felt almost like tearing my hair in desperation—it wasn't that I wanted to insult the girl. If I had made that remark, every single word would certainly have turned back on me like a sharp knife and stabbed me in the breast. Hadn't I already felt hurt inside, even without actually making the remark? The fact is, I wanted to insult myself. Wasn't this sort of insult the most appropriate parting gift to myself now I that was destined to go to my death in a strange place without ever having known the warmth of a woman's love, having only made a thorough job of wasting my youth.... Sitting there by the window, I stared fixedly at the girl's attractive profile.

"You frighten me!"

The girl turned aside slightly, as if to avoid my gaze. She seemed to give a faint shudder. For a moment the right half of her face was illuminated in the feeble electric light. Her cheek went right up to the edge of her hair. The place where the ear should have been attached was pale and smooth, like the place on a plant where the fruit has been taken off.

"What have you done to your eyelid?"

"I fell down a cliff."

"That was nasty, wasn't it?"

I stood up and took off my jacket. And time went by. During this short period of time—just enough for me to become aware of the decline in my physical powers, and not at all pleasurable—my mind was far away, on other things. I had come to this town on a small train. Early the next morning I would leave it on a bus. I had never been to the town before and would never come again. How far would my night in this dilapidated brothel signify the closing off of the paragraph which was my youth. I lay talking to the girl, listening gloomily to the noise of freight trains passing below the window.

"You're going to Sakurajima, are you?" she asked, her head buried against my chest. "It's a nice place! There's fruit growing all the year round. When you get there now, there'll be pears and tomatoes. It's a bit late now, perhaps, for the loquats."

"But I'm in the Navy. There may be a lot of fruit, but that doesn't mean we'll be able to eat it as we like."

"I suppose not. . . .what a shame! A real shame!"

The girl looked up and burst into a fit of laughter. But she stopped at once and looked hard at my face.

"And you'll die there, I suppose?"

"Yes, I shall die. What's wrong with that?"

She went on looking at my face for awhile, and suddenly, speaking as though to no one in particular, she burst out, "I wonder when the invasion will come."

"Before long, I expect. Very soon, in fact."

"You'll be in the fighting, won't you? And be killed in action?" I said nothing.

"You're going to die, aren't you? How will you die? Come on, tell me! What sort of death will you die?"

I was listening to the sound of the wind, which seemed to be blowing right through my breast. The girl's strangely solemn face was close to my chest. Until the time came, I couldn't possibly know how I ought to die. At that moment death seemed peculiarly close. I could not repress a shudder of deep foreboding, but I returned the girl's gaze with an assumed air of unconcern.

"Stop asking unpleasant questions!"

Her face had the lackluster appearance of paper–but not her eyes, which made me feel uneasy, staring fixedly at me. The right side of her face was pressed tight against the pillow. Her face looked small, about the size of a mandarin orange.

"Let's both stop talking about such unhappy things."

"But I *am* unhappy! I *am* unhappy!" The girl's eyes seemed to have filled with tears. I shut my eyes. I was suddenly overwhelmed by an almost painful surge of tenderness. I felt as if I had to grit my teeth as I lay stroking the girl's cheek with my hand.

The next day, in drizzling rain, I reached Taniyama. The inside of the dugout was damp throughout, and the air was foul. The cipher room was at the far end of the dugout. Carrying my rain-sodden, heavy cap in my hand, I went in, bending over to avoid knocking my head. It was so hot that however many times I wiped my glasses, they kept misting over again at once.

"I want you to leave right away for Sakurajima. There's no cipher P.O. there."

"There ought to be one there, surely, sir."

"Yes, but he's in Kirishima Hospital with dysentery."

I was talking to the officer in charge of cipher personnel.

"I will leave at once, sir."

Coming out of the cipher room, I saw some P.O.'s and enlisted men that I knew by sight, and we said hello to each other. They told me that they'd been having a long spell of rain, and that two or three days before, the entrance to the dugout where they had their living quarters had caved in. The earth here was sandstone and not very firm. The inside of the dugout smelled very unpleasant, possibly because of the damp. The men all looked very pale.

There were six enlisted men who had been due to go from Sasebo Naval Barracks to Sakurajima, but had come by mistake to Taniyama, and I was told to take them with me. So the seven of us formed up at the entrance to the dugout, reported to the duty officer, and marched off through the drizzle along the dirt road to the local streetcar stop. I discovered that the six men were all reservists, and were being sent for repair work on human torpedoes and suicide attack boats.

"Has Sakurajima got suicide attack boats now, then?"

"I don't know, sir."

It was the oldest of the six, a seaman first class who had answered. He looked over forty. He was a wretched sight in his illfitting work-uniform. His kit bag was very small, too. Having lost everything in the fire at Sasebo Naval Barracks, he said, they had only been issued with a bare minimum of clothing. When he saw how heavy my kit bag looked, he kept offering to change with me and carry mine. He seemed a decent type of fellow, but his naive insistence on following Service custom I found rather irksome.

"I'll carry my own," I said curtly, and for the rest of the way marched on in silence. We reached the streetcar stop. We got on a small streetcar and seemed to have gone hardly any distance at all before we had to get off. Because of the bombing, the streetcars were not going any farther. Again we formed up and marched off, this time on a paved road.

The city of Kagoshima was half in ruins. Nothing retained any shape but the shells of ferro-concrete buildings; apart from these, the scene was one of rubble-strewn desolation. Here and there broken hydrants spouted white columns of water. Telegraph poles were down and the cables trailed along the pavement. Here, too, rain was falling, like swirling ash. At the end of the ruins there was the sea. Across the water towered the grim mass of the peak on the island of Sakurajima, swathed in a brownish mist of rain. "I'm going to the foot of that," I thought. We all marched on without a word. My kit bag was heavy on my shoulder. While we were waiting on the quay for the boat, the sky at last began to brighten. The clouds broke up and allowed blue sky to show through. The people waiting for the boat were all rather stupid-looking and didn't talk much. The girls at the ticket office were eating steamed potatoes. It strangely stimulated my appetite. I avoided looking at them and sat down on my kitbag, watching the expressionless crowd. I was thinking about the girl I had had the night before. The emotions of that night seemed to be clinging to me with a curious persistence. These feelings almost of tenderness produced the opposite effect in me, provoking a sense of disgust with the faces of the stolid crowd on the quay. (They were as expressionless as horses.)

I clicked my tongue loudly. My party had persuaded the girls to share the potatoes with them and were eating them furtively, trying not to let me see them. Time crawled tediously by. In due course, the boat came in, setting up a surge of foam-flecked waves. We went aboard. The boat moved off through the dirty water.

Presently we reached the opposite shore, the gangplank

was let down onto the sandy beach and people passed along it one by one and jumped off. This was Sakurajima. My unit was at a place called Hakamagoshi, about two-and-a-half miles' walk along the coast road. I looked up to find the sky clear and streaked with vermilion in the evening light. I began to feel much brighter myself and more at ease. I even had a cheerful word for the men, and marched my party off. Trees stretched away into the distance, following every twist and turn of the road, their foliage bright green after the rain. We called at what looked like a farmhouse and bought a lot of pears.

They were small, hard pears, light brown in color. Afterwards, I noticed the light-brown fruit of these wild pears dotted here and there among the clumps of trees.

"Are these the pears that girl was talking about last night?" I wondered, biting into them and spitting out the skin. They were neither juicy nor sweet.

The sun went down. The chirruping of the swarms of crickets all over the mountain subsided. We reached our unit while it was still dusk. There was a line of seven or eight huge caves in the cliff which rose precipitously from the road, each clumsily camouflaged with such things as dead branches. There were any number of oil drums and other things lying around by the entrance to the dugouts. And there was a stream of men in and out—all older men. I could hear the gentle lapping of the waves.

I went to see the duty officer and handed over the movement order for my party of seven, then I left the other six. An enlisted man from signals came along and I set off with him for the living quarters. Those for the signals personnel were near the top of a hill. As we walked up the dark, difficult mountain path, I looked up at the sky. The branches were so intertwined that I could not see the stars.

"Is it still farther up?"

"We're nearly there, sir."

We came out onto a fairly wide path where the branches were no longer interlaced overhead. On one side was the cliff, with a view out over the dark sea. I felt a faint breeze on my eyes. Across the sea lay the black mass of Kagoshima, with just one place where there was a fire sending up red flames. To me, in my exhausted condition, the fire seemed to have an odd, unearthly color; it burned dully and slowly.

"There are fires like that every night, sir." I felt strangely moved at the man's words.

We went down to a narrow path and reached the living quarters. The entrance, somewhat smaller than those of the caves at the foot of the cliff, had the same irritating camouflage of bamboo and trees, while a large number of cables trailed over the face of the rock. The dugout seemed to be U-shaped. I stooped and went in.

The farther end of the dugout was the transmitting office and was cluttered with generators and transmitters. There I met several people, including the senior signals P.O., and reported. The passageway to the signals office was arranged to serve as living quarters, with rows of bunks and tables. At one of the tables a warrant officer was sitting with a bottle, drinking saké by himself. He appeared to be a big-boned man but there was very little flesh on him, and he had the sallow complexion characteristic of signals personnel. His bloodshot eyes, above gaunt cheeks, were fixed on me. He had one hand resting on a stout sword such as army officers wear, and the fingers round the saké cup were unnaturally long.

"Petty Officer Murakami?"

I saluted.

"Duty here's tough, let me tell you. I don't allow anybody, under any circumstances, to get out of night duty just because he's a P.O. I don't know about other bases, but this place at least is the front line. Every day the Grummans come over. We're all going to die here anyway. Until we do, don't do anything that will make people talk about you or make you a laughingstock.

His voice was hoarse, like that of an old man.

"Very good, sir."

"As for me, I'm Chief Petty Officer Kira."

The moment he had barked this out, as if flinging the words at me, he suddenly shifted his gaze, which had been so firmly riveted on my face, and did not deign to look at me again. He fixed his gaze on the empty air, having apparently completely forgotten me, and raised the saké cup to his lips with his long fingers.

"May I go now, sir?"

I saluted and was taken by one of the men to my allotted bunk. Stuffing my kitbag underneath it, I took off my damp uniform. From the bottom of the hill came the faint sound of the bugle for inspection. The bunks were in two tiers, and the upper one had a new wooden tag attached to it, with "P. O. Murakami" in very bad writing. I climbed the ladder and stretched myself out on the blankets. Above my face as I lay on my back ran a number of cables and bare wires, which gleamed dully in the dim electric light inside the dugout. A continual shower of fine sand seemed to be falling from the roof. I lay there with my eyes shut.

(Those eyes!)

What was this uncanny look in the eyes which is never found except in enlisted men? They had a maniacal gleam behind them. They were not the eyes of an ordinary person. They were the eyes of a degenerate. The shudder which ran down my spine when our eyes first met—was it not the first sign of my terror? As he gradually learned what I was thinking and feeling, Kira would inevitably come to hate me. That I knew by an invaluable intuition, acquired in over a year's service in the Navy. The possessors of eyes like those never failed to see into my character, and without exception hated me.

"I'll have a tough time with him," I whispered aloud. How long this life at Sakurajima would continue, I didn't know. But at the thought that all the while I was living there, that is to say, till the very moment of my death, I would have him as a superior officer, I experienced a vague, bitter sense of foreboding.

The memory of the previous night seemed like something

which had happened long, long ago. It was a far-off world to which I could never return.

After a time I appear to have dozed off and fallen into a deep sleep.

That was how my life at Sakurajima began.

There was a system of two watches a day and three at night, with another, from 6 p.m. till inspection time, which could be counted neither as a day nor as a night watch; the arrangement was for this to be taken by those who had been on duty in the morning. So on days when you were on duty longest, you were on for twelve hours out of the twenty-four. That does not mean that there were many messages, of course. The level of technical skill in signals personnel and the quality of cipher personnel had dropped steadily, so much so that some of the cipher personnel could not even manage to decode one complete message in a six-hour spell of daytime duty. Of course, that was perhaps not surprising since the cipher personnel here were largely volunteers, including some, even, who were only fifteen years old. Another unfortunate thing was that when not on day duty, they were all put to work digging dugouts. The result was that on night duty they would all sit dozing over their work, and a message would be passed on uncompleted every time they changed over, and sometimes would still not be finished by the morning. The blame always fell on the P.O. on duty.

The cipher room was in the same dugout as the receiving room, halfway up the hill. Possibly because it had been badly located, it was very damp, and the atmosphere was terribly stuffy. When you went in to take over, it made you feel sick, the air was so foul. Consequently it was proposed to dig a hole in it for ventilation. There was no doubt that it was a good idea to construct this hole for ventilation and for introducing a cool breeze, but one day while I was on the spot supervising some of the men from my watch who were working at it, I made a calculation and found that it would be at least three months before the ventilation hole was finished. About November there would indeed be some very cool breezes blowing in, I thought with some annoyance, and I said to one of the men, "Who ordered this work?"

"C.P.O. Kira, sir."

"He thinks this place will hold out as long as that, does he?"

The man lay aside the basket he was carrying earth in and came and stood in front of me.

"Will the Americans invade before this hole is finished, sir?"

His face looked solemn. He was one of the teen-age cipher personnel, going on fifteen years old. I took a deep draw at my cigarette and asked, "Do you think we'll win?"

"Yes, sir, I do."

That face showed not a trace of doubt, just like a character in the world of fairy stories. I suddenly felt depressed and motioned to him to get back to work. I must have looked very disagreeable at that moment. I stood up and crushed out my cigarette with my foot. And I walked away.

Walking up a gentle slope, I found the top of the hill thinly wooded with tall trees; as I went along the path which threaded its way through them, the afternoon sun beat down on my face and the sweat poured off me incessantly. Emerging from the trees, I came to a fairly big field. A large chestnut tree grew in the center. Beneath it was an enlisted man, who looked round in astonishment at hearing my footsteps.

He was a short man around forty, and I suddenly noticed the binoculars he had in his hand. Seeing me looking at him rather suspiciously, he gave a friendly little smile and said very distinctly, "I'm the lookout, sir."

Indeed, there was a telephone fixed to the trunk of the chestnut tree, and this field commanded a panoramic view of the bay and the sky. Through the heat haze that shimmered over the grass, I went up to the man.

"Would you lend me your binoculars, if you're not using them?"

"Certainly, sir. By all means use them."

I took the binoculars. They were very heavy. I put them to my eyes and slowly traversed the field of view.

Directly before my eyes was a headland formed by lava which had flowed down into the sea as a result of the eruption that took place about 1913 or 1914. This side of it was the harbor square, with a water tower in the middle, looking like some medieval turret. I could see soldiers clustered round it drawing water or doing their washing. And I could see the sea, as calm as if oil had been poured on it—motorboats in the harbour—and then as my head moved round, the whole mass of Mt. Sakurajima came into the field of the binoculars. It was devoid of any trace of vegetation, just a pile of enormous red-ochre-colored lumps of rock, a formidably huge mound of red volcanic material. It was beyond calling a mountain. It may have been the effect of the lenses, but the shadows on the face of the rock stood out very sharply and overwhelmed my eyes with the might of inanimate nature. As if bewitched, I could not take my eyes off it.

"Excuse me, sir."

The voice sounded low and suppressed. Automatically giving up the binoculars, I looked at the man's face. He was in a half-sitting position, watching and listening intently.

"It's a plane, sir."

As he took the binoculars from me, he looked at the sky to the south. I could hear nothing. There was only the raucous downpour of the cicadas' chirruping.

There wasn't a cloud in the sky. The sun was shining brilliantly, moving round with imperceptible slowness. There were signs that somewhere in this sky, cleaving its way through the wind, a plane was approaching.

The man took the binoculars from his eyes and dashed to the telephone on the chestnut tree. He rang the bell. It sounded curiously unreal when heard on a hill like that.

"One Grumman. Yes, one Grumman, over Kanoya. Course . . . course north-northwest. . . ."

At that moment—quite suddenly, it seemed—a clear metallic sound came to my ears, though still only very faintly. Just as I was about to look up at the sky, the man took hold of my elbow.

"Take shelter, we've got to take shelter, sir!"

About five yards away from the chestnut tree, beside a clump of shrubs, was a slight depression in the ground, and hurriedly we scrambled into it. The two of us lay side by side on our backs. My heart was pounding.

"This is my coffin, sir," the man said quietly, and gave a faint laugh. Indeed, it was the shape of a coffin. It was too narrow for two. I turned myself round towards him to make some reply, and in that instant a metallic sound which seemed to tear the air asunder suddenly swelled to an explosion, and came over my head in one ear-splitting surge. Gleaming silver, the great shape of the Grumman flashed into my view and instantly was gone. Instinctively I began to sit up, and just as I did so there came the rending crash of a burst of machine-gun fire. Then it stopped. The noise of the plane's engines receded in no time and appeared to die away out at sea. The chirruping of the cicadas, which I had forgotten while the plane was passing over, now burst out again. The man picked himself up and went to the phone.

"Plane retiring in the direction of Kagoshima. Yes, it's gone away."

After awhile we heard the all-clear siren from far down at the foot of the hill. I got up and stood among the flowers in the field, looking round at what lay below. Men who had just been sheltering in various places gradually began to appear on the road and in the square.

I flung myself down and sat on the grass next to the man.

"I suppose the Grummans often come over."

"This is the first time today, sir."

The man glanced at my face and said, "Are you a conscript, sir?"

"No, on the reserve."

"Did you take the P.O.'s exam?"

"That's right. I didn't want to, but. . . ."

"It's better than being an enlisted man, though, isn't it, sir?" he said, and laughed nervously.

"Lots of cicadas about, aren't there?"

"They're chirruping even at night sometimes, sir."

"There are none of those *tsukutsuku-bōshi** ones yet, I suppose?"

"Not yet, sir. Not till about the middle of August."

A flicker of agitation seemed to me to pass across his face.

"Horrible things, aren't they, sir, *tsukutsuku-bōshi* cicadas?" he said, and then, after a pause, went on, "They're my pet aversion! Every summer, when they begin to chirrup I'm always unlucky. It's a funny thing to say but . . . last year, I was called up on the first of June. And I went to Sasebo Naval Barracks, I expect you know, sir, the Tenth Division. Well, every day we had such a lousy time to put up with there that I got very depressed about how it was all going to end. Then one day we were on cookhouse duty and we were lined up outside the place when the first *tsukutsuku-bōshi* of the year landed on a tree nearby and set up his damned chirruping. It was just after Saipan fell, and we'd been told by the squad leaders that whatever happened, our unit would be fighting to the last man in the South."

He broke off for a moment.

"The year before it was the same, sir. And the year before that, too. Whenever I had some misfortune or hardship and I was feeling fed up with life, the *tsukutsuku-bōshi* would start chirruping. Their chirrups are horrible, aren't they? A bit like a human voice, don't you think, sir? Strange, like their tune meant something. They're not really cicadas, you know, sir. I don't feel too happy when I think about what moment they'll choose to start chirruping this year, either."

---

* Meimuna opalifera. The Japanese name is onomatopoeic.

He was silent for awhile.

"How did you become a lookout, then?" I asked.

"I took a course for it in the autumn. It wasn't easy, in many ways."

"Particularly when you're not so young as you were, eh?"

"It wasn't only because of my age, sir."

"You didn't get much sympathy, I suppose."

He said nothing.

"It's the volunteers. Volunteers who've risen to be P.O.'s or C.P.O.'s. Those guys haven't got a shred of feeling in them."

He nodded. And in a low, mournful tone, he said, "Until I went into the Navy, I'd never come across anybody without feeling, and it was a real surprise, I can tell you, sir. Feeling is something they just haven't got. They think they're human, but they're not, are they? Something that a normal man has to have in him dies out completely in the course of life in the Navy, and they become like ants or something, without any feeling or will."

"Mm, mm."

"They come in as volunteers. They get squeezed dry, just as you squeeze an oil cake, and they lose something that's vital. They become P.O.'s. They take the process a few stages further. Then they get three or four good-conduct stripes and eventually they're C.P.O.'s. At last they've got a living. They get married. From then on they spend their time looking forward to being handed a Special Duty commission or the like and working out what their pension will be, or dreaming about building a little house on Sasebo Bluff to live in after they've retired. The fact is that this sort of life is ensured at the cost of everything that is most valuable in a man. Can you think of any other life as hard as this? You lose your humanity to get a living. Is it impossible to live without going as far as that? So just look at them, these C.P.O.'s. They either become completely hopeless louts, or they become all dried and shriveled up."

"Yes, you're right."

I was picturing C.P.O. Kira. He was neither shriveled nor a lout. He was a man of a completely different stamp. In all probability, all the while he had been tormented with the punishment stick, from the time when he first volunteered, he had unconsciously nurtured a pathetic feeling of vengeance where other men would have resigned themselves and submitted passively. He had probably fostered and cultivated the extreme cruelty which is latent in men's hearts, and extended it even to himself. When he eventually became a C.P.O. and was able to feel more settled and took stock of his position, he had probably realized that the fangs of vengeance which he had fostered had in fact no role to play: he had no one to sink them in save himself. This was perhaps the reason for his strange disposition, his queer behaviour, and the irritability he developed when the fighting in Okinawa ended with his whole world, the Navy, in ruins.

There was a very clear picture in my mind of his eccentric behaviour in getting the men in signals together for quite unnecessary punishments. This had happened two or three days before....

Dysentery was rife. That day, one of the cipher personnel had picked and eaten some wild pears and then had been sent off to Kirishima Hospital with suspected dysentery. The eating of pears was strictly forbidden by the M.O. I had left the man in the sick bay and was eating my supper back in the living quarters. I was eating some pickled fish–little thin ones that they seem to catch in the bay–when someone passed behind me and turned round. It was C.P.O. Kira.

"P.O. Murakami, what's the matter with Yamashita?"

"He's been sent to Kirishima, sir."

"Is it true that he'd been eating pears?"

"Apparently, sir."

Yamashita was the name of the sailor in question. An angry look appeared on C.P.O. Kira's face.

"Haven't the men been told time after time not to eat

pears? The men are a slovenly lot nowadays, but they're all good enough at doing what they're not supposed to." His voice sounded rather choked. Staring me in the face, he said, "The P.O.'s are at fault as well. Because they're slovenly, the enlisted men do as they like. If they don't want to obey my orders, I'll teach them how to. P.O. Murakami, fall the men in."

I said nothing. It made no sense that because one man had eaten some pears, all the rest should be punished. In the few days that I had been living here, I had begun to feel a certain affection for the cipher personnel under me. I didn't want to have them punished for no reason at all. My expression did not change and I remained obstinately silent. C.P.O. Kira suddenly turned aside and strode off into the transmitting room.

I turned back and went on with my meal. Since I had been called up, I had spent some time as an enlisted man in all the units at Sasebo Naval Station and the Sasebo signals unit and the Ibusuki air unit. Memories of all kinds of humiliations were still fresh in my mind. There were countless unpleasant memories which it made my blood boil even to think of. The terrible thing was that I could clearly see that I was on the way to acquiring an attitude of servility.

(And now that I was going to die, what did all that matter?)

I felt very depressed as I finished my meal. I left the dugout and went down the path in the evening sunlight to the cipher room. And I took over the watch.

There were not many messages. There was nothing of any importance in the day's file, only messages reporting, for instance, that one *Ginga* plane was leaving such-and-such a place, or that goods had been sent by truck to so-and-so. The assistant cipher officer on duty was dozing in his chair. All around, the noise of transmitters could be heard. Half the telegraphers were from Primary Flight Training School. They had been assigned to signals because of the shortage of training planes. Sitting chin on hand, I closed my eyes. . . .

. . . A short while before, when I had been coming down the path in the evening sunlight, an antiquated training plane had been flying over, above the peaceful bay of Kagoshima. It was doing no speed at all, absolutely crawling across the sky, with its wings fairly shaking. I had heard two or three days before that the suicide bombing squadrons were using these training planes. After that, I felt I wanted to shut my eyes, but I couldn't help looking. I was visualizing the young pilot sitting in that plane.

I opened my eyes. I had seen some Naval suicide pilots while at the Bōnotsu base. They lived in the National School, some distance away from the base units. Once I had passed their place. In front of the National School, there was a building like a tea shop, and in front of that stood a bench where two or three suicide pilots sat drinking saké. They were all youngsters of about twenty. Their white silk mufflers looked strangely inelegant. They all had coarse complexions and wild expressions. One of them was singing a popular song, in falsetto, and in a rather suggestive way. It sounded thoroughly unpleasant to me as he would come out with something and they would all laugh. So these were the suicide pilots!

They gave the impression of young men from the country just into adolescence. Wearing their caps on the backs of their heads and their white mufflers tied in a dandyish fashion, they looked all the more like clodhopping yokels. As I stood looking at them from a distance, they turned and scowled at me, shouting, "What're you looking at, you bastard?" They must have thought I was a new recruit in a construction unit.

It is difficult to say whether the feeling which mounted within me was sadness or anger. This was one feeling, at any rate, that I was quite unable to deal with, that has left a nasty taste in my mouth, and that I still have even now. It was possible for me to imagine that people who faced death gladly did not always do so for the noblest of motives and in ideal surroundings, but what I had just seen at close quarters was somehow rather disgustingly redolent of the purely physical man. As I walked back with bowed head towards the base, I was thinking of nothing but how to live a beautiful life and, when the time came to die, how to die in a way that left no regrets....

Suddenly I came out of my reverie and looked round me. Besides myself, there were only two of the men at the table in the cipher room. In the remaining place, someone had left a thick "B" code book and a coding board, set up ready, but no one was there.

"What's happened to this watch? It's long past the time for changing over, surely?"

One of the men looked up and answered, "They all came, sir, but...."

"What happened, then, if they came?"

"They were sent for from the living quarters. Anybody with messages in hand was to stay, but all those who had nothing to do were to report there."

"Who sent for them?"

"C.P.O. Kira, it appears, sir," replied the man, a little nervously.

Even I could feel that my face was tensing up.

The man who exercises direct control over the men is the petty officer. It was not the fact of having my authority over the men in this respect set aside that annoyed me. Now that it was only a matter of time before this place became a battlefield, where was the need for comrades-in-arms to hurt each other? That made me feel utterly miserable. The two men with me knew quite well what was happening to their comrades in the living quarters. For no other reason than that they happened to have been decoding messages, they were getting out of it. Looking the picture of misery from feelings of guilt and a vague uneasiness, they were thumbing through their code books. A feeling of uncontrollable disgust made me begin to lose my temper.

"Right! I'm going to the living quarters to see what's

going on," I whispered to no one in particular, and stood up. I went along the narrow passageway and found it already dusk outside. I ran up the mountain path, and just as I began to take the lateral path downwards, I came to an involuntary halt. At the entrance to the living quarters dugout stood C.P.O. Kira. And in front of the dugout, on the slope overlooking the sea, the men were all down on the ground in the "Arms bend" position. C.P.O. Kira, with a three-foot stick in one hand, was bellowing at the top of his voice at the men who were trying to let their bodies sag in the middle and touch the ground. I approached, walking more slowly.

It was clear to me from their slack attitudes and the desperate efforts they appeared to be making to change their hands to a more comfortable position that the men had been holding the posture for a very long time. Every head was drooping. In the twilight I could quite clearly see sweat dripping off the forehead of the man by my feet. I felt as if I were choking. I had been made to do the same thing many times. My elbows being weaker than most people's, I had always had to endure twice as much pain as anyone else. The memory of that linked up with the scene before my eyes, and I felt as if I could hardly breathe. I stole a glance at C.P.O. Kira's face.

In the poor light, it looked so pale that it gave me a start. A strange expression, as if he were fighting against extreme pain, seemed to distort it. His eyes alone, blazing like those of a maniac, moved to and fro over the backs of the prostrate men. The pupils were the color of fire. All at once he turned round and looked at me.

"P.O. Murakami. Tell the men to stand up," he flung out at me, and threw his stick away down the cliff. Thudding two or three times on the edges of rocks, it fell down into the bamboo-covered valley. He stood still, looking as if he wanted to say something to me, but he said nothing, turned his back on me, and strode off into the living quarters. Somehow there was an air of loneliness about his broad, thin shoulders.

"On the feet, up!"

Slowly and wearily the men all stood up. They all had the same naive look, possibly from exhaustion. They were, so to speak, like caged animals in a zoo, bereft of all capacity for thinking. With a strangely ominous feeling of oppression, I said in a low voice, "Men on duty return to your posts, remainder dismissed."

I set off with the men on duty along the path to the cipher room. Only on the surface of the sea was there still a faint trace of twilight; among the clumps of trees it was dark. Had C.P.O. Kira expected me to get the men on their feet and then give them a dressing down? Or had it been sufficient for him just to have inflicted pain on them? I did not know. The back view of him as he disappeared into the living quarters, walking as though dragging some heavy weight behind him, remained in my mind's eye. It could not in his case be anything so simple as it was with other P.O.'s, that is, doing to the men exactly what they had had done to them when they were enlisted men. It seemed that some impulse lurking like a chronic disease in his mind drove him on. Some kind of devil, something that was beyond my comprehension and perhaps even beyond his, seemed to be running amok in him.

(That was the explanation of those eyes!)

The P.O. who had been my squad leader when I was undergoing recruit training had also had eyes like that, though his disposition was quite different. Usually he was quite mild, then suddenly he would have a fit of cruelty. Later, I had heard, he got into some trouble or other and was court-martialed. Recollections of this man now flashed across my mind.

In the final analysis, these were men who lived in an entirely different world from mine. And I was too exhausted to understand the devil in C.P.O. Kira. Or rather, not exhausted but too concerned with my own imminent death to think about such irrelevant matters. The distant vague threat of death had been with me constantly, ever since I had come to Sakurajima.

Without doubt I was on edge. Lack of sleep for days on end was partly responsible. But that was not the only reason. In a word, I was unable to believe in my own destiny. This island in southern Japan—which I had learned about in geography lessons at school, it is true, but could hardly have expected ever to have any cause to visit—why should I have to come here and be compelled to die here? That was what I could not comprehend—or rather, could not persuade myself to accept. It was not something you could accept. But the situation was pressing. I had come to the point where somehow, in some form, I had to resign myself to my fate.

Occasionally, the conversation in the cipher room and the living quarters would get around to the question of where the U. S. forces would invade. It was plausibly rumored that the Navy anticipated a landing at Fukiage-hama, while the Army was concentrating all its main force on the defense of the Miyazaki coastline. The last-ditch defense of Okinawa was already over, and the sortie of the *Yamato* had ended in failure. Our overwhelming defeat was clear from the code messages which we deciphered every day. Judging from the American planes flying over day after day, a landing was certain to come in the very near future. August came, in a calm that was pregnant with an ominous tension. During the night of the first of August, I was on duty.

Under the dim lights of the dugout, which smelled of bare earth, the men were all busy consulting code books, their eyes glinting sullenly. Every now and then a sleepy-eyed runner came in from the signals office with a message. The sound of the pages of the code books being turned was curiously irritating. I reached out and picked up the message which had just been brought in. It was Operational Top Priority. I gave a start and raised my head. Surely something had happened at last. Hurriedly I flipped through the code book. Word by word, I wrote the message down on a Decoded Message Form.

"Enemy convoy 3000 ships sighted. Course N."

It was a signal sent out by the lookout station on the island of Ōshima. I stood up.

"Message about an enemy convoy, sir."

A momentary look of tension passed across the sleepy face of the duty officer.

Electric bells sounded, the operations room was informed immediately, and the chief cipher officer, cipher officers and signals officers who had been asleep in the row of bunks along the passageway to the cipher room were roused by the men and came trooping in. As they entered the cipher room, they all screwed up their eyes and tried to look away from the light. They gathered round the O.C.'s table, talking in low voices.

Suddenly the volume of messages grew. Every one was Operational Top Priority. Reports, information dispatches and orders radioed to all units were apparently going back and forth all over Japan. The convoy was clearly heading for the Tokyo area. Weren't they perhaps going to attack along the Chiba coast and in one stroke capture Tokyo? It was not impossible. The population of Tokyo was at this moment presumably asleep, knowing nothing of all this.

Suddenly I had a vivid recollection of Hongō, where I had been living till I was called up, and of my friends. These were quiet streets and peaceable people; quite unconnected with the war. The misfortune to which I had resigned myself as destined to fall on me was now about to be transferred to them. Would they not be blissfully asleep in their beds, ignorant of these monstrous evil tidings of death. A certain thought suddenly crossed my mind, bringing with it a sharp stab of pain. If they land at Tokyo, doesn't that mean that I won't be killed, being here at Sakurajima?

I felt like groaning as I pursued this thought.

The voices round the O.C.'s table behind me gradually became louder. Occasionally people laughed. Amid the tension, curious feelings of desperation grew more and more involved and became magnified, till a slightly forced note seemed to come into the joking voices.

"Those people on the General Staff and in Eastern District signals who thought they were in a good berth will have a bit of a shock."

"It's a bit late now for 'em to complain about having made a big mistake."

"Still, there's plenty of room to escape in the Kantō Plain, surely."

Someone put in, "It looks as if the suicide units will be going out to attack."

For awhile no one spoke. The silence bore down on my back till it hurt. At that moment, someone threw out a casual joking remark.

"What's it matter, anyway? This time next year we'll be working carting American flour. In Sasebo harbor or somewhere."

Several of them laughed quietly.

"There won't be any "enlisted men" or 'C.P.O.'s' when that happens."

Suddenly someone cut off the conversation, in a quite different tone of voice, completely unamused.

"Stop talking damn nonsense!"

It was a serious, emphatic voice. The laughter ceased. I twisted round slightly and glanced furtively behind me.

"Stop talking in that disgraceful way in front of the men."

It was C.P.O. Kira. When he had come into the cipher room, I don't know. Feeling that I could hardly go on staring at him, I turned back and pretended to be consulting my code book. He appeared to have stood up as he spoke. In the chill which had fallen over the room, I heard someone say, "He was only joking, wasn't he? It was a joke, that's all."

He was trying to restrain Kira.

"No one thinks Japan's going to be beaten, or anything of the sort."

"C.P.O. Kira, stop making a fuss when there isn't any need."

I heard a half-incoherent gasp of "What!" followed immediately by what seemed like a struggle. There was a dull thump as of flesh against flesh, then someone staggered and fell on my back as I sat hunched forward. The coding board clattered to the floor, and thirty or forty of the numbers were scattered around. I felt heavy breathing on my neck. I stiffened my back, and went on staring at my code book. I thought I heard a kind of hollow laugh. Involuntarily I turned round. The tall figure of C.P.O. Kira was leaning up against the wooden framework which braced the dugout, his face waxen, drained of blood and with a mask-like expression. Instinctively I looked away, feeling as if I had seen something that I ought not to have seen, and at that moment C.P.O. Kira spoke, in a low, almost groaning voice.

"Stop, please."

It was hard to tell whether he meant "stop making jokes" or "stop these undignified quarrels"; his voice sounded feeble, as if he were talking to himself. An icy silence fell. During this silence C.P.O. Kira apparently went lurching out of the dugout. The sound of his jackboots on the damp earth followed. And I could feel on my back the atmosphere of relief after tension. I was flipping aimlessly through the day's message file. My fingers shook as I turned the pages, however hard I tried to stop them.

(A convoy had been sighted. That alone was enough to make everyone excited.)

I felt an utter disgust rising within me at this bunch of men, myself included, who had so lost hold on themselves. Or rather, not disgust, but a feeling more akin to anger. A feeling of wanting to tear myself limb from limb, and them along with me, and hurl the pieces down into the valley. I struck myself several times hard on the back of the neck with my penknife. Each time the blood rushed up to the back of my head, bringing on a tingling sensation.

"P. O. Murakami. P. O. Murakami. Decoded message for your inspection, sir."

It was one of the men speaking. I put out my hand and took the message. It was transcribed in very poor, childish handwriting.

"Earlier report mistaken. For 'enemy convoy,' read 'patches of phosphorescence.' Ōshima lookout station."

A wry smile came to my lips. Wasn't it all a farce? If the Americans were monitoring Japanese radio communications, what must they have made of this sudden storm in the ether—this mass of Operational Top Priority messages, from Ōshima to Yokohama Naval Base, from Yokohama to all parts of the country, from unit to unit. Not long before, our own unit had received the order to stand by from Sasebo Base. The maintenance personnel must now have been roused and be getting down to work. What would they feel like when they went back to bed after learning that there was no convoy, but only patches of phosphorescence instead. My smile grew more and more pronounced, like some physiological spasm, completely beyond my power to control. I got up and presented the message to the duty officer. All the C.P.O.'s and others at the C.O.'s table fixed their eyes on it. Not one of them laughed, though, on reading it.

"So that's what it was," said someone in a strangely flat tone.

I went back to my seat, and heard the duty officer calling up the operations room on the telephone. The line was evidently bad, for he seemed to have difficulty in making the person at the other end understand about the phosphorescence. At the same time I was listening to the other C.P.O.'s who were talking wearily among themselves.

"He seems to have been strung up lately, doesn't he?"

"The poor man's got a bee in his bonnet, that's what."

There the conversation ended. Since there was no longer any reason to stay up, they all left the dugout for their respective sleeping quarters.

Three o'clock came. The next watch arrived to relieve us. We handed over the books and left the cipher room together. As I emerged from the passageway, it was pitch black. To accustom my eyes, I leaned against the cliff by the entrance and waited awhile. As usual there were fires burning slowly at one or two points in the city of Kagoshima, on the opposite shore; it seemed no one bothered to put them out any more. Dull fires were burning in the same places, and sending up the same volume of flames as on the previous night.

I set off. As I walked along with some difficulty, feeling with one hand for the cliff, I was imagining the swarm of phosphorescent organisms which had been mistaken for a big convoy. When I visualized their tiny purple gleam, shining from one end of the dark ocean to the other, curling about like a belt and moving slowly along, my mind felt cleansed and refreshed. Though I knew quite well that it was a reaction from my earlier mood, I let myself wallow in this sentiment. A quiet feeling of isolation was spreading pleasantly over me. The night wind blew against my face.

I made my way very slowly up the path and reached the living quarters. As I entered, someone was sitting leaning on a table at the far end. He looked across at me. It was C.P.O. Kira. He looked as if he had been sitting quite still like that for some time.

"Are they near their landing point?"

"I understand it was only patches of phosphorescence, sir," I replied, undoing the collar of my work uniform. A peculiar expression, neither relieved nor puzzled, appeared momentarily on his face, and was gone again. It was something like the pained expression on a child's face when it is bullied. I was not sure because he had his back to the light. And then he closed his eyes.

Going to the sleeping quarters, I lay down, trying to avoid making any noise. I covered my face with both hands. My eyelid was still itching constantly. The injury I had received at Bōnotsu was almost healed, and the scar seemed to form a wrinkle. As I rubbed the place with my finger, the nail made a scratching noise against the rim of my glasses. I lay listening to it, feeling miserable.

I finished my morning watch and at noon returned to the living quarters. While on duty, I had been reprimanded by the cipher officer in charge of the watch. I had been late in handing over a message. It was a monitored message, anyway, and had no connection at all with our unit. The duty officer had probably only wanted to raise his stock with the operations room. Very depressed, I finished my meal, then turned in and had a nap. And I had a dream.

I don't remember what the dream was about—only that I was walking in some place where it was half-dark, shrieking at the top of my voice. I was wandering along aimlessly, with tears streaming down my face. I was shouting, all the while swinging my arms and stamping my feet. In the meantime, I slowly came to the surface, as it were, and I woke up. I was soaked with sweat. My whole body felt dull and heavy, and in parts of me the sensations I had had in my dream still persisted. Though I was now awake, the tears still streamed down my face as in my dream. I seemed to want to cling to something, and lay still on my bunk, enduring the unpleasant clamminess of my skin.

(Could I let this go on? Could I....?)

A wave of revulsion at being unjustly treated was agitating my half-drowsy mind. I had worked up a solitary rage. Not about anyone in particular. Not about the chief cipher officer. I felt violently angry with whatever had driven me into these straits. Suddenly an acute sadness came over me. Wasn't it vain effort, all of it? How many times had I had such feelings of emptiness pile up within me, only to break them down again?

I sat up and jumped down from the bunk. As I put the edges of the rumpled blankets together to fold them, I suddenly whispered, "Even blankets have ears."* What

* The Japanese word for "ear" also has the meaning of "edge, border."

unhappiness and bitterness that country prostitute must have suffered, through missing an earlobe! That night the girl had lain with her face nestled against my chest and told me scraps of information about her life. How at school she had been called "No-ears." How, when she had sold herself into prostitution, having an earlobe missing had forced her to come to that sort of wretched country teahouse. Faced at every turn with such injustices, what had enabled the girl to keep up her spirits through life? I suddenly recalled the sight of her mournful profile. And following this, bringing a sense of utter wretchedness, came the recollection of her skinny figure.

(Clinging to such sentimentality and making my feelings independent of my surroundings—was that the only way to calm my agitation?)

My youth was over. My life at Sakurajima was now nothing but a matter of living out the rest of my days. Automatically my hands busied themselves putting the folded blankets into an untidy heap, then I dressed and left the dugout. The strong afternoon light flooded into my eyes. I decided to go and have a look around at the top of the hill.

I went up the stony path and through the wood to the lookout post. Under the chestnut tree stood the same look-out as before. When he recognized me, he seemed to smile faintly. He looked somehow in low spirits.

"It's you again, sir."

Nodding, I mounted the lookout platform, and gazed round in all directions. The brillant sunlit scene was enough to cheer me up completely.

Cumulo-nimbus clouds hung in the sky. They were massive pillars soaring up to a height of several thousand feet, and glittering silver. Down below them I could see the airfield of the Kagoshima squadron, and on it the tiny shapes of the smashed hangars and fire-reddened iron girders. The scorched and blackened city stretched away to the east. The mountains around the city were a beautiful blaze of vivid green, but over towards Taniyama hung a white pall of dust, and there was a blurring haze over the bare clay where part of a hill had been cut away. Only Nature was beautiful. The ruins of what man had made were twisted and ugly. I sat down on the grass. The man sat down beside me, as he had done on the previous occasion.

"Even lookout duty's quite a tough job, I expect."

"There's nothing much to it, sir."

"You look depressed, somehow. Don't you feel well?"

"I'm tired, sir, that's what it is."

He indicated the peaceful bay with a sweep of his hand.

"There are three submarines in this bay, sir."

"Oh yes, I saw that in one of the messages. But aren't they ours?"

"In signals, are you, sir? No, we don't really know whether they're ours or the enemy's."

"People are saying they'd forgotten to put up any sign to show they were ours."

"Oh?"

The man was silent for a moment, then he asked, "If you're in signals, sir—those boys in the suicide unit, how are they getting on?"

"No good at all. They all appear to be knocked out by the Grummans."

"They really are no good then, sir?—It's pretty awful for them, these suicide pilots, isn't it?"

"Awful? What is?"

The man was silent for a moment. Then, speaking as if he had to keep a check on every word, he said, "You know that story about Kiso Yoshinaka, sir—how he let some oxen loose into the enemy camp with torches tied to them. Those oxen—that's what the suicide pilots are. When I think of that, I feel really sorry for the young men in the suicide units—going to their deaths, without knowing why."

"I suppose you have children yourself?"

"Now and again a formation of training planes goes over. I suppose they're suicide planes as well?"

"Yes. . . ."

The man's face looked very sallow—perhaps it was the effect of the light. He seemed utterly worn-out.

"You'll have to take care of yourself, you know. Living in dugouts takes it out of you."

"Long ago it appears there was a race of people in Kagoshima called 'earth spiders.' Something like the Kumaso. They were the same as us, living in caves."

"You come from Tokyo, don't you?"

"They're died out now, sir. They were probably a weak race."

"What a lot more cicadas there are! So many that they're a real nuisance."

"Bear-cicadas" were perched on trees here and there, chirruping as hard as they could.

"Cicadas? Oh, the cicadas. The *tsukutsuku-bōshi* hasn't come yet this year."

He laughed nervously, showing his white teeth. He was very slim about the shoulders, which the set of his jacket made to look boyish. A vague uneasiness took hold of me. The man lay back with his hands linked behind his head. There seemed to be no planes coming over today. The man began to talk in a low voice.

"You know, sir, lately I've been thinking about the beauty of destruction."

He spoke carefully, and as if he were speaking to himself.

"Ruins are really beautiful, aren't they?"

"Can you call them beautiful?"

"I have a feeling that along with the will to live, people have a will to move towards their destruction. I can't help feeling that that's so. Amidst all this vigorous life of Nature, man goes feebly to his death, like a moth. In a strange kind of way, it's beautiful, don't you think, sir?"

The latter part of this became almost a soliloquy.

"I saw a very strange sight recently, sir."

"What was that?"

He handed me his binoculars and pointed at the valley over to one side.

"You see that house over there, sir—that farmhouse? A

bit more to the right. Yes, just there. Have a look at it through the glasses, sir. At the side of the main building there's a shed, isn't there? From the eaves of that there's something hanging, isn't there? Can you see it?"

Through the binoculars I saw a long object like a cord, hanging from a beam over the entrance to the ramshackle shed, and swinging backwards and forwards in the breeze. A child crouched on the ground in front of the shed, playing. What all this was, and what it meant, I didn't know. As I gave the binoculars back, I looked at the man's face.

"Well? . . . ."

"That house belongs to a peasant family, sir. They appear to have a paddy field or a dry field somewhere quite a distance away, and every day the man and his wife seem to go off with mattocks and things. There's an old man living there, and he seems to have been ill in bed for a long time in a room at the back of the main building. Sometimes he comes out to go to the privy beside the shed, but really he's very helpless. Even through the glasses, you can see that he's unsteady. On top of that, it looks as if he's been ill for a long time, and he appears to be treated as if he were in the way, because he often gets a nagging from the woman when she comes home to get the dinner ready. Then there's a child, a flat-headed boy of about seven or eight, and he seems to make fun of the old man, too. Of course, I'm only seeing them through glasses, so I don't hear what they say, but I could tell from this pantomine, by what they did, and—well, that's the situation. The child makes fun of the old man, but he's the old man's grandchild, after all, so he's made a fuss of."

"You seem to know a lot about them."

The man gave a hoarse little laugh.

"That's what I guess the situation to be. Well, looking at it from the old man's point of view, he's made to feel in the way by his son and his daughter-in-law, and he has nothing to look forward to—so one day when I was watching from here through the glasses—it was in the middle of the day and scorching hot—he crawled out onto the veranda, then stepped down into the garden and walked over to the shed. I watched him, thinking he was going to the privy, but it appeared he wasn't. With a lot of effort he brought a stool and a rope from inside the shed. Just as I was wondering what he was going to do, he put the stool by the entrance and tried to get up on it. But he was so helpless that he fell off two or three times and went full-length on the ground. I got so terribly agitated that I even found my hands sweating as I held the glasses. Then finally he got on the stool. Clinging to the beam, he tied the rope to it, then he made the bit that was left hanging down into a noose, and gave two or three slight tugs, evidently to test its strength."

"He was going to hang himself!"

"Finally he must have been satisfied. He looked all around him. And there was that boy, standing directly behind him, about six feet away, like a ghost. Not saying a word, he was watching closely what the old man was doing. You could see from here that the old man was shaken. He stood looking round at the boy, staring at him, without letting go of the rope. The boy, too, was as motionless as a rock, eagerly watching the old man. For about ten minutes, they remained eying one another and not moving. In time the old man collapsed and fell off the stool onto the ground. The boy still did not move, and made no effort to lend him a hand. Crawling over the ground across to the veranda, the old man lay face downwards on the stone step, and judging from the way his shoulders were shaking, he lay for a long time sobbing his heart out. For an awful long time."

The man half sat up.

"You saw that just now, didn't you? That was the rope."

I felt a sudden dislike for this man. Not for any definite reason. In a slightly spiteful tone, I asked, "It must have given you a nasty feeling, I suppose?"

"Cruel–that's the word for how I felt. What was cruel? Was it the fact that the old man was driven to do such a thing? Was the boy watching cruel, or was it cruel of me to have been observing such a private scene secretly, through glasses?—I don't know. I have a sort of feeling that I was grinding my teeth as I was watching."

The man raised his head and stared at the sky. The sun hung in midair, shining brilliantly.

"I wonder now. Can it be that people are not able to die with someone else watching? Is it only possible to die when alone?"

He put a hand up to shade his eyes from the glare. With the strong light falling on it, his face looked half-smiling, half-crying.

When I came off watch in the evening and went outside, the sky was bright with clouds lit up by the glow of evening. The men who had just come on duty said that there had been a beer ration issued that day, and some of them had rather red-rimmed eyes. While I had been on duty, just before I was relieved, an urgent message had come in. I had decoded it.

I was thinking about that message as I went back to the living quarters. Its contents were decisive.

When I entered the living quarters, I found a long row of tables down the middle of the passageway, with all the men seated on both sides and a line of beer bottles standing on them. The whole place was full of tobacco smoke, and you could hear the clink of bottles on glasses. I made my way to the far end and took my seat. As I watched the beer being poured out into my glass. I felt somehow incapable of entering into the spirit of this rowdiness. The tables were stained with white froth. I took off my tunic and lifted the glass to my lips. The tepid liquid went down my throat with a pleasantly heavy sensation.

The senior signals P.O. and C.P.O. Kira were sitting in front of me. The P.O. was red in the face, but Kira looked if anything rather pale. And my attention was caught suddenly by his voice.

"Huge reinforced concrete buildings were completely wiped out, they say."

"Completely, sir?"

"It looks as if they had a rough time."

"Where, sir?"

"Hiroshima."

I was listening casually. C.P.O. Kira suddenly turned to me.

"P.O. Murakami. Have there been any messages?"

His bleary eyes seemed to flash fire. The message which had come in before I came off duty crossed my mind again.

"Russian troops have crossed the frontier, sir."

My words apparently gave him a considerable shock. But his expression did not change. Without a word, he drained his glass. Agitatedly, he drummed two or three times on the table, quite meaninglessly, with his long fingers.

"They've joined in against us, eh?"

"I don't know about that. In the message it only says hostilities have begun, sir."

I was looking hard at C.P.O. Kira's face. A semblance of a smile appeared on his expressionless cheeks. A cruel smile, enough to make your flesh creep. Instinctively, I averted my eyes. I tipped up my glass and poured beer down my throat. Once again I tipped up the bottle and poured some into my glass. A feeling of intoxication gradually seemed to be working round me. A delicious feeling of languor spread through me, in which it seemed my extremities were being detached from my body.

The talk at the tables some distance away from me became louder and louder. The men were stripped to the waist, and beads of sweat were running off them. Over by the entrance the evening light was beginning to fade. I felt I didn't care what happened, and leaning with my elbows on the table, I went on and on pouring and drinking.

Gradually my intoxication spread until I began to feel rather dizzy. Confused thoughts kept streaming into my mind and out again. I was thinking vaguely of Bōnotsu. Things had still been all right at that time. The girl clerk at the Bōnotsu Post Office had given me twenty postcards as a parting gift because I was being transferred. They were tucked away at the bottom of my kit bag. So far, I hadn't used a single one....

I suddenly had a sharp twinge of conscience. Since coming to Sakurajima, I hadn't even written home. My old mother was probabaly not even aware that I had come to Sakurajima. My brother was in the Philippines, in the Army. He might not even be still alive. My younger brother had been killed in Mongolia. Suddenly a savage feeling came over me, like a blast of wind. What had the Japanese nation achieved, with all these sacrifices? If you were going to call it wasted effort...if it was wasted effort, at whom should I direct my shouts of anger?

The chatter in the dugout was growing more and more raucous, then suddenly, at a table near the entrance, someone burst into song, very much out of tune, and a number of others joined in. The song was "Cherries Blooming Together." The bottoms of beer bottles were being banged on the tables. The singers—high voices and low voices all together—changed to a new song. Leaning on the table, I could feel the vibration through my elbows every time they banged on it. I was aware that my eyes were becoming set. I poured out still more beer, and drained it at a gulp.

C.P.O. Kira, who appeared to have been sitting in silence steadily drinking beer, twisted round to face me. He was already stripped to the waist. His tough-looking, muscular shoulders were glistening with sweat. He addressed me in a low, provocative voice.

"Did you say to the men that the war would be over by the end of this year? Eh, P.O. Murakami?"

"I have said nothing of the sort, sir."

Those hateful maniac's eyes were fixed on my face. I decided to act casually. The hand in which I was lifting my glass to drain it shook a little.

"I may have said something to the effect that if things go on like this, with one desperate battle after another, the losses will be so great on both sides that neither will be able to carry on for long."

As I spoke, I felt a sudden rush of anger at my own

weakness. I stared back at him, and said, "It doesn't matter very much, does it? A silly thing like that....?"

"Will it be over this year?" His tone was insistent. His speech seemed a little slurred. "P.O. Murakami. Are you afraid of death?"

"It doesn't worry me, sir."

"You are afraid of it, aren't you?"

I moved so close to his face that I could quite clearly see the red veins in his eyes. Intoxication made me bold. My face felt cold as ice as I answered clearly, pronouncing each word distinctly, "I suppose you would be satisfied, sir, if I were afraid?"

For a moment Kira's eyes seemed to fill with hatred. It was only for a second. Something told me not to get up. I remained seated. C.P.O. Kira bent his head back and burst into a convulsive laugh. His voice was laughing, but his face was not. By now my clenched hands under the table were sweating.

One of the men got up from his table and staggered up to us. The singing was a confused blur of sound.

"I'm going to do a dance, sir."

"All right, do a dance!" said C.P.O. Kira, suddenly ceasing to laugh and speaking in a tone almost of rebuke.

Stripped to the waist, the man assumed a curiously contorted position of the hands, then suddenly broke into a terribly quick, haphazard kind of dance, calling out to mark the rhythm. Pivoting on his tottery legs, he spun round like a top. With his hands curved like a cat's claws, he stretched up and bent down, all the time calling out the rhythm. The singing stopped and was followed instead by hoarse laughter.

"What the hell's that?"

"Stop, stop!"

The man gradually went faster and faster. He flung himself about like one possessed, his eyes closed, though whether this was because he was dizzy, or because the sweat streaming from his forehead got into them, I could not tell. He staggered and supported himself against the wall of the dugout. A faint cloud of dust rose into the glare of the electric lamps. With a nonchalant expression, he saluted.

"That's all, sir. It's a dance from Shikoku."

Singing started afresh. Ribald remarks seemed to be flying about, but I could not hear properly. Some distance away there was the sound of a beer bottle breaking. And a ragged chorus began.

> Farewell then, Rabaul,
> My eyes are filled with tears,
> For I must say goodbye,
> Until I come again.

I shut my eyes. My heart was thumping violently. I supported my chin on my hand. My face felt rough because of the dust on it. I had a dull headache. My thoughts were concentrated on one thing.

I was not afraid of death. No, it was not exactly that I wasn't afraid. To speak frankly, I hated the idea of death. But if I was to die anyway, I wanted to know why. To die like an abandoned cat on this island along with the insect-like men living here, surely that was too sordid. Never having been blessed with anything worth calling happiness, I had worked hard and assiduously to build up something—which was now to be buried completely in the mire. But what was wrong with that? Was that a bad thing? Without realizing what I was doing, I found myself talking to C.P.O. Kira.

"C.P.O. Kira. If I'm one of those to die, then I intend the moment of my death, at least, to be a beautiful one."

A cruel smile rose to his lips. He spoke maliciously, as if taking me to task about something.

"Look here, I've seen action all over the place since I joined the Service. I was in China. And in the Philippines, P.O. Murakami. Imagine a hail of bullets over scorched fields. We're a marine unit advancing through the midst of it. Every time a bullet whistles across, you feel as if it's going through your forehead. You look for a lull in the racket and run like mad. If one bullet hits you, you know, you get knocked over with terrific force. Everybody else moves on and you're all alone in the open, out in scorched fields, struggling along all by yourself. Before long you can't walk and you stop breathing. Your face is all twisted up, and dirty streams of blood congeal in the mud. Night comes, then the dawn, and in the evening thousands of crows gather, pecking at your flesh and strewing it around. There are thousands of maggots, too. Soon night comes on and a chilly rain falls, washing the bones of your arms and your backbone white. Nobody can tell any longer who you are and where you come from. Nobody can tell whether you're a corpse or not. You want a beautiful death, P.O. Murakami? You want your death to be beautiful?"

As he finished, he burst into a horrible laugh, enough to make my flesh creep. I was keeping a firm hold on myself and thinking of Lt. Tani. That young, lively lieutenant had also told me it was nothing but sentimentality to want to die a beautiful death. But what did that mean? Only that nihilism had bitten deeply into Lt. Tani's and C.P.O. Kira's souls. What relation did that have to my own secret longing to die a beautiful death?

A strange sadness came over me. I did not look at C.P.O. Kira again, but stared vacantly at the table. The rowdiness seemed to be growing. Flogging on my increasingly befuddled senses, I poured some more beer down my throat. Something which had been troubling me for some time, and which I had unconsciously suppressed whenever it threatened to raise its head, suddenly appeared to be taking clear shape in my mind. What had I been living for? What?

This "I," what was it? For thirty whole years since my birth, I had been attempting, you might say, to discover what this "I" was. At some times I had viewed myself conceitedly as above average, at others I had looked down on myself as quite worthless; my life had consisted of fluctuations of joy and sadness between these two extremes. When the time actually came to die—and it was already close at hand—what attitude would I take, now that I had abandoned all pretence and bluff? Would I run away when a steel bayonet was levelled at me for the purpose of destroying this individual called "I"? Would I grovel and beg for mercy? Or would I stake all my pride and fight? What I had been seeking for thirty years would become clear in that moment. I was less afraid of the enemy than of the approach of that moment.

(You're going to die, aren't you? How will you die? Come on, tell me! What sort of death will you die?)

When that prostitute without an ear had asked me this, her voice had sounded partly as if she were crying and partly as if she were restraining a fit of laughter. Behind the singing noise in the ears which drinking had brought on, I had the illusion of hearing her voice once again quite distinctly. Tilting my head back, I leaned against the wall and closed my eyes. In my head was the chirruping of cicadas. Thousands and thousands of cicadas were chirruping away madly inside my skull....

This queer party in the dugout grew more and more frenzied, and excitement reached fever pitch. As a breeze blew in from the entrance the singing was taken up again. The tables shook. I opened my eyes. The Soviet Union had entered the war–so what? I shook my head vigorously two or three times, and in an effort to escape from my previous mood, I thought I would join in the singing. I put my hands on the table and tried to get up, cautiously putting my weight on my unsteady legs. C.P.O. Kira's voice rang out through the dugout like a blast of wind.

"Men. Fetch my sword!"

He was obviously too drunk to know what he was doing. His eyes were set, and his face frighteningly pale. He tried to stand up but lost his balance and leaned on the table with one elbow. A beer bottle fell over with an almighty clatter, and white froth dripped onto the floor. With one hand on the table, he stared at his subordinates.

"Fetch my sword. I'm going to do a sword dance."

He reeled forward. Above all the hubbub someone began to chant a Chinese poem in an animal-like grunt.

Who it was, I couldn't tell, and it was impossible to make out words or tune clearly. Still, Kira drew his sword. There were three or four handclaps, but they soon stopped. There was some laughter. A second voice joined in, and the chanting became very ragged and uncertain, proceeding by fits and starts. With his sword held up in front of him, C.P.O. Kira swayed backwards and forwards from the waist. He suddenly opened his eyes wide. He swept the sword down close to the wall, and as he straightened up he carried his fist on up to his eyes. He overbalanced and clutched at my shoulder. The sword dropped from his hand and fell noiselessly onto the earth.

"Murakami. Have a drink! Have another drink!"

My shoulder was almost numb with pain under the grip of his hand. I shrugged to try to ease it, and put out my left hand for another bottle of beer. . . .

I went down the hill and did my washing under the water tower in the harbor square. It was very hot, without a single cloud, but there was a steady breeze blowing from the southeast. The washing seemed likely to dry quickly. There was a crowd of men round the water tower doing their washing, hardly any of them young. I heard the man washing his clothes next to me say to another, "They say the Soviet Union's come into the war, don't they?"

"Yes."

They said no more. The man addressed looked rather disgruntled. The lather they were washing with floated along the gully in front of me, a billowing white mass.

Seeing that the Kagoshima newspaper office had been burned out, there could hardly have been any newspapers brought into the camp. I had heard the chief cipher officer forbid the men to pass on the news about the Soviet Union coming into the war, but in spite of that it had not taken long to get around. There was a slight "go-slow" feeling prevalent in the unit. It was impossible to put your finger on anything definite, but it could be sensed, like a smell of decay. The officers were spending all day lazing under

M. KUWATA

awnings erected by the side of the coast road, and even the men, going in and out of the dugout with baskets of earth, moved very sluggishly.

Walking along the coast road, I climbed the hill with my bundle of washing in my arms. I carefully hung the washing out on the trees in front of the living quarters. We would have trouble if it could be seen from the air. I went into the dugout and took some notepaper from my kit bag. I sat down at the table, spread the paper in front of me, and sat thinking hard. After awhile I wrote on the first line of the paper, "Will." I laid my pen down and stared at the wall in front of me.

I couldn't think of anything to write. I felt that there were plenty of things I wanted to write about, but when it came to the point it was all rubbish. The will was not addressed to anyone in particular. I grew more and more annoyed. I stood up, tore the paper into pieces and threw them away.

As I left the dugout and walked to the top of the hill, a feeling of sadness came over me. What was my object in writing a will? I had wanted to make an appeal to someone. But about what? I had wanted to convey to someone a sadness not yet framed in words, a sadness which when put into words became false. This may be called an act of sentimentality, but what does that matter if in the course of it I found some relief?

The path came to an end and I entered the wood. This was the way to the lookout post. Perhaps the healthy view from there would take my mind off things. I looked up at the sky. The light penetrating the network of branches fell on my face in patches.

Suddenly I pricked up my ears. Amid the rain of chirruping from the cicadas, I heard something that sounded like engines. I ran to the edge of the wood and looked up at the sky. From one corner of that great bright sea of deep blue, a sharp, metallic sound came cutting through the air. A dark spot appeared. In no time it grew bigger and took on the shape of an airplane, apparently flying straight towards me. A foreboding of danger swept over me. They must be going to attack here! I ran into the wood, on and on, panting for breath. The horrible, terrifying sound of engines approached faster and faster and swelled in my ears. With sweat streaming from me, I was trying to run still farther into the wood when the plane, now apparently directly overhead, judging from the noise of its engines, suddenly opened fire with its machine guns with a paralyzing roar. Instinctively, I dropped and pressed myself flat on the ground just as the great black shadow of the aircraft came skimming over like a hurricane.

I lay face downwards, my eyes tight shut. My heart was thumping so madly that it was almost more than I could bear. I seemed to have a lump sticking in my throat. Gasping for breath, I opened my eyes. The smell of the earth by day struck my nose. The sound of engines receded.

Slowly I got up and dusted myself off. As I wiped the sweat away with my sweat-cloth, I looked up through the branches at the sky. The plane had apparently already disappeared in the distance. I set off walking.

On the previous occasion when I had seen the Grumman from the lookout post, I had admittedly been shaken but I had not felt scared. What was the strange fear that had seized me now? What was the awful dread that had set my teeth chattering?

My gloomy thoughts of the last few days concerning death must have left their mark—some crack, as it were, in my mind. Thinking about death must have had the opposite effect of fanning my desire to cling to life. As I went up the path near the lookout post, I was smiling grimly to myself.

(People about to make a will run around in a cowardly fashion, like lizards, trying to escape death.)

A bitter feeling of self-derision came over me.

I reached the lookout post. I looked all around but couldn't see any sign of my lookout man. All at once, I noticed something white beneath the chestnut tree.

(Was he still sheltering?)

Puzzled, I went closer. There under the chestnut tree, the lookout man lay prone, quite motionless, as if he didn't hear my footsteps. His hands, stretched out on the ground, were somehow unnaturally twisted. The visible side of his dust-stained face was curiously pale. I stopped aghast. I had seen the virulent red of bloodstains on the grass. Feeling as if I had been doused with cold water, I stood rooted to the spot, dumb with horror.

About halfway up the trunk of the chestnut tree against which the corpse was lying, the first *tsukutsuku-bōshi* of the year was chirruping quietly, persistently, sounding off its ill-omened tune like some messenger from hell. Suddenly my eyes filled with scalding tears.

(He must have heard this chirruping of the *tsukutsuku-bōshi* as he died!)

I went down on one knee and tried to lift his body. The head rolled round slackly. He had a slight growth of beard and his closed eyes looked so sunken that I could scarcely recognize them. The bullet had penetrated his forehead. The stream of blood from the wound went as far as his temple. There was no sign that he had felt any pain. Between the slightly parted lips I could just see his discolored teeth. He felt unnaturally heavy on my arm, as I wiped away my tears with the other hand.

To the end I had not heard his name, or his circumstances, or his birthplace. As far as I was concerned, he was to be no more than a chance acquaintance. Wasn't his exposition of the beauty of destruction a way of reconciling himself to the fact that he would have to die here? Probably, being frightened by a premonition of misfortune, he had been telling himself over and over again of the beauty of destruction. Probably he had been at pains to devise some reason for his premonition of death, and had been trying hard to believe in it.

(How could destruction possibly be beautiful?)

My jaws tight-set, I laid the corpse on the ground. Why had he abandoned any desire to survive? Having talked himself into the right frame of mind, he had in the end died with no regrets, the sound of the *tsukutsuku-bōshi* cicada in his ears.

A gust of wind faintly stirred the beard on his unshaven chin. The corpse seemed to be wearing a smile. Suddenly I felt a strange, powerful surge of emotion within me—not a feeling of closeness to him but not one of hatred, either. I stood up. I saw the shadow of my own unsteady self fall across the corpse lying there beneath the chestnut tree.

Taking a deep breath, I walked towards the telephone. I picked up the receiver. A voice suddenly burst on my ear. "What's happened to the Grumman? Has it gone yet?"

"The lookout man is dead, sir."

"What? I'm talking about the Grumman. Why haven't you reported sooner?"

". . . . The lookout is dead, sir."

With that, I replaced the receiver.

I picked up the man's cap. Squatting down beside the corpse, I covered his face with it. I stood up. Holding my breath, I moved across and quick as a flash caught the *tsukutsuku-bōshi*, which was still chirruping insistently. The regular rhythm changed in my hand to confused squeaks. The wings, whirring with tremendous speed, gave me a painful sensation, as of burning, on my sweating palm. Was there so much strength in this newly-hatched, feeble insect? I suddenly had an urge to treat it cruelly. Squeezing it as hard as I could in my hand, I put it straight into the pocket of my uniform. The fluid from the cicada's body felt revolting as it spread over my palm. I steeled myself against the feeling as I stood looking down at the man's dead body.

Nobody had come up yet from the bottom of the hill. A slight dizziness spread from the back of my head, and I shivered.

The order had come out that morning that since the Emperor was going to make a speech over the radio, everyone not on duty was to listen. As I had seen more or less all the messages relating to our unit, I knew all about this, but not having read a newspaper or listened to the radio since coming to Sakurajima, I was quite out of touch with the outside world. So I did not fully understand the significance of an Imperial broadcast. In the sense that it was entirely without precedent, though, I could imagine that it must be something serious. Uncertainty made me feel on edge.

Being on duty in the morning, I was unable to go and hear the broadcast. As soon as I came off duty I went back to the living quarters. The broadcast was being relayed in the square at the foot of the hill. Everyone must have been there listening. Even when I had finished my meal in the living quarters, the men who had been to hear the broadcast were still not back.

"That broadcast's taking a long time!" I thought to myself.

I lit a cigarette and went to the dugout entrance. Down in the bay I could see little waves, and all around the *tsukutsuku-bōshi* cicadas were chirruping. The sun was hot, but somehow there was a hint of autumn in the air. I looked and saw men coming back to the living quarters in twos and threes. The broadcast was evidently over.

"What was the broadcast about?" I asked, grabbing a young signalman who was just going into the dugout.

"The radio wasn't very good, sir, and we couldn't hear."

"There was a lot of interference and we couldn't catch a thing, sir," added another man.

"Still, it was long, wasn't it?"

"After the broadcast, there was a talk by the C.O., sir."

"What about?"

". . . . He said we were all too slack and lazy and out for naps on the sly. But if we won the war, we'd surely be able to have all the rest we wanted. Serving the country was required now, or not at all. That's what he said, sir."

" 'If we won the war?' Did he say that?"

"Yes, sir."

The men saluted and went into the dugout. I threw my

cigarette away over the cliff and set off towards the cipher room.

The previous day the chief signals officer had come into the cipher room and inspected the code books. Since it was impossible to foretell when the enemy was going to land, he said, it might be better to burn all code books not needed much, so as to avoid any confusion when the time came. The burning was due to take place that afternoon. I intended to be present myself.

As I approached the cipher room, I met two or three signalmen coming out, each carrying a heavy-looking wooden box on his shoulder.

"Are those the code books?"

"Yes, sir."

We walked up the path which went right to the top of the hill. I walked back up alongside a fellow P.O. from signals who was bringing up the rear of the party carrying a bottle of gasoline.

On the opposite slope to the lookout post on the other side of the wood there was a small hollow, and there the men had dumped the wooden boxes and were sitting wiping the sweat from their faces. As we approached, they stood up and began to take the code books out of the boxes. The books were piled up in the hollow, all of them red-covered, some big and some small, some well thumbed and some new.

The signals P.O. went round to the other side and poured gasoline all over the pile. I struck a match. Blue flames leaped up, the red covers began to curl up like living things, and soon they were a mass of red flames. I felt a slight catch of regret in my throat. I spoke to the signals P.O.

"I wonder what that broadcast was about today."

"I don't know, they say it was probably an Imperial command to defend Japan to the bitter end."

"Who said that?"

"The O.C. signals, for one, and C.P.O. Kira said something to that effect, too."

I stood watching the flames. Occasionally, according to how the wind blew, I felt the heat on my face. For awhile the thick code books would seem to be smouldering and not burning properly, then the pages would curl over again and flames would leap up afresh. Thin clouds of smoke drifted with the wind across the sky. The smell of burning cloth hung about. From time to time there was a noise of something splitting in the fire and a shower of sparks flew up.

"They'll be landing any day now, I suppose."

Someone poked at the code books with a stick, pulling them nearer, and fresh flames rose again. The smoke billowed up more thickly.

"If you make too much smoke, we'll be for it when the Grummans come."

"There won't be any coming today. After all, there weren't any yesterday, either."

This meant that the Grummans had not put in an appearance since the day the lookout man was killed—neither yesterday nor the day before. The fact that no aircraft had come over suggested that invasion was imminent. The enemy had probably given up random attacks and were organizing for operations in force. Whether the point where they landed was Fukiagehama or the Miyazaki coast, we here would have our line of retreat cut off in any case.

Even if we took refuge in the mountains, the range was hardly deep enough for us to make a successful getaway. In particular, this was a Naval suicide unit base, so that after the human torpedoes and the suicide boats had left on their one-way journey, we should no longer have any duty to perform. What kind of orders would be given when the time came, seeing that the men didn't even have rifles?

I was idly watching the color of the flames. They looked transparent in the daylight. The hilltop was completely still. Only the splitting noises in the fire broke the stillness. The voices of the men talking to each other sounded curiously distant. Beyond the trailing smoke Mt. Sakurajima towered like a giant. A sense of peace and calm came over me as I looked at the shape of the mountain.

What did it matter if our line of retreat was cut off? Let me stop thinking about anything. Even if I could not meet death with composure, let me die a death true to myself. What took place and how things developed in Japan after my body was buried and reduced to inorganic matter no longer had anything to do with me. Let me live unhurried, calm, until my death.

"P.O. Murakami. Shall we burn the wooden boxes, too?"

"Yes. Burn them."

Noisily the boxes were broken up and flung one after another into the fire. With this new fuel, the flames flared up like long strings of sticky amber candy. I put my hand casually into my pocket. Something crackly touched my fingers. I took hold of it and pulled it out. It was the dead body of the *tsukutsuku-bōshi* cicada which I had caught a few days before. It was completely dried up and one of the wings had broken off. As I turned it over on my palm, it made a crackling noise. Furtively, so as not to be seen by the others, I threw it into the fire. It disappeared into the ashes of the charred code books.

Are they true, I wonder, those tales, made up by people who have not died, that a man recalls the whole of his life in the moment of death, or that even though the body dies, the brain lives on for a few seconds and experiences agonizing pain? The face of the dead lookout had been peaceful, but it was not the face of a man who had learned in death the key to all the mysteries of human life. In death he had looked commonplace, no longer a serviceman, but like any ordinary person. For some reason I remembered very clearly the dirt on the collar of the tunic he had been wearing when I lifted him up....

By dusk the code books had been completely burned. We beat the ashes to make sure that nothing had been left unburned, and then went back to our quarters.

As I went in, C.P.O. Kira was sitting down at the far end. Holding his sword up with one hand, he was drinking something from a mug—apparently alcohol and water. I could faintly smell it.

"Have you burned them all?"

"All finished, sir."

Hanging the tunic in my hand on the bunk, I went towards the table.

"You there!"

A signalman who appeared to be tidying his kit bag hurried over to him.

"Go to the cipher room and ask them if there's been any message about His Majesty's broadcast today."

The man saluted and hurriedly left the dugout. There was no one else present. Just C.P.O. Kira and myself, alone in the dugout. Everyone else had gone off as usual, apparently, to dig the hole. I sat down opposite the C.P.O. He stared back at me in his usual way. He spoke hoarsely.

"They'll be landing any time now, P.O. Murakami."

"Was that what today's broadcast was about, sir?"

"That I don't know. There's been no change in the state of the enemy for the last two or three days. That proves he's planning large-scale operations. You're prepared to die, I suppose?"

He gave a mocking laugh.

"If they land, what will happen to this unit, sir?"

"It will make a grand sortie, of course."

"No, I don't mean the suicide units, sir. I mean the construction and signals men who are left."

He looked suddenly annoyed, and looking me in the face, drained his mug.

"They'd fight!"

"What would we do for weapons, sir? On top of that we've got a lot of reservists and militiamen over forty. . . ."

"The reservists would fight, too."

His tone was lashing.

"There are bamboo spears."

"Have they had any training, sir?"

As he watched me, a fierce glint suddenly came into his eyes. I mustn't be afraid of him. I would act naturally. Determined on that, I stared back at him.

"They don't need any training. They'll go in as suicide

troops. P.O. Murakami, here you are stationed at a base for Naval suicide units and you still don't understand the spirit of the thing?"

"I think it might be better to give them some training than make them dig a hole which won't be finished till God knows when."

I felt hot all over, and spoke with great emphasis. C.P.O. Kira stood up straight. Almost leaning on me across the table, he said, "I will not have you criticizing my policy, Murakami! When I want your advice, I'll ask for it."

An inexpressibly deep sadness suddenly swept over me. Feeling as if something was disintegrating inside me, I bent backwards, looking steadily into Kira's eyes. He thundered down at me, "Do you think we'll win if the enemy lands?"

"I don't know, sir."

"Do you think we will?"

"We may. But...."

"But?"

"Japan was beaten on Luzon. Okinawa was wiped out. You can't tell whether we'll win until the time comes...."

"Right!" shouted Kira, cutting me off short. It was like an animal bellowing. He fixed his eyes, glinting eerily like glass balls, straight on me.

"Here's what I'll do when the enemy lands....take this sword and..." he thumped the top of the hilt heavily with one hand "....go round cutting down all the cowards one by one. Murakami! I'll hack them down wholesale. Have you got that, Murakami?"

Involuntarily I made to stand up, and just at that moment the signalman, returning from his errand, came in like a ghost through the entrance to the dugout. He came straight up to us. Coming to attention, he put his head back and saluted smartly. He spoke clearly.

"The broadcast today was an Imperial proclamation of the end of the war, sir."

"What?" I shouted automatically, half-rising from my seat, with my hands on the table.

"It was an Imperial proclamation, sir, that the war is over."

A queer shudder ran through me from head to foot. I felt my right hand on the table begin to tremble. I turned round and looked at C.P.O. Kira's face. All expression had gone out of it, and I saw his lips tremble slightly as he tried to speak. He said nothing. He just collapsed onto his chair. I distinctly saw tears rolling down his thin cheeks. I turned back to the signalman.

"Right. I'll go to the cipher room at once. You go on ahead."

I left the table. I was so agitated that I felt unsteady on my feet. A mass of emotions too confused for me to be able to disentangle them surged up inside me and died away again. Just as I began to walk over to my bunk where my tunic was hanging, I was conscious of something like a phantom behind me, and I turned round.

Under the feeble electric light, C.P.O. Kira sat facing the rough table, leaning on his sword and staring with vacant eyes at the wall. On the table the mug stood empty and undisturbed. The transmission room at the far end of the dugout was lost in the gloom.

I turned away and went to my bunk. I took my tunic down to put it on. For the second time I had the feeling of something incomprehensible and mysterious pressing close to me from behind. Instinctively I turned round.

C.P.O. Kira had not moved from his position of a few moments ago. The scene was exactly the same as it had been—the cables running along the roof, the mug on the table, the grubby walls. I put my tunic about my shoulders and made to walk over to the exit. As I put my arms into the sleeves and fastened the buttons one by one, I suddenly felt alarmed by an atmosphere of strangeness. Gripping the edge of my bunk, I turned round for the third time.

Sitting before the table, C.P.O. Kira had drawn his sword from its scabbard. He brought the blade close to his face. The thick blade, catching the feeble electric light, shone brightly. He was staring at it as if bewitched. There was an aura of ferocity about his whole body. In the slightly bent back, in the eyes, like those of a hungry animal, I saw a brutal will which was not of this world. I stood leaning on my bunk, my eyes fixed on him. A strange excitement set my whole body trembling. I was aware of the faint noise which my knees were making, knocking together. I stood there with eyes wide open while time went by, a ghastly time during which my blood seemed to freeze.

C.P.O. Kira moved. Guided by his hand, the blade, gleaming hypnotically, was put away in its scabbard. I heard the sword-guard strike the scabbard with a hard, clear sound. The sound went right through me. C.P.O. Kira altered his grip on the sword and stood up, looking at me all the time. And he spoke to me softly, in a pathetic voice. I did not budge as I listened to him.

"P.O. Murakami. I'll go with you to the cipher room."

As we left the dugout, the sea was bright with the reflection of the glow in the evening sky. The path disappeared into the fading dusk. C.P.O. Kira walked ahead of me. Above the cliff was the peak of Mt. Sakurajima, tinged by the setting sun. The mountain face, now visible and now hidden by the trees as I walked along, had an ethereal beauty with its light and dark patches of color, red and blue. As I hurried along the stony path trying to keep up with C.P.O. Kira, scalding tears suddenly streamed from my eyes. Again and again I wiped them away, but they fell in an endless flow. The landscape, through my tears, became distorted and disjointed. I clenched my teeth and walked on, fighting back the choking sensation which rose in my throat. My mind was a confused jumble of thoughts and nothing was clear anymore. I did not even know whether I was sad. Only, my eyes brimmed with tears, again and again. I covered my face with my hands and staggered on step by step down the path.

Translated by D. E. Mills

Haruo Umezaki was born in Fukuoka, Kyushu, in 1915. He graduated from Tokyo University, majoring in Japanese literature. His activities as a writer did not truly begin until after World War II, although his first novel was written in 1939. He served in the navy signal corps and was stationed at Sakurajima, the title of this short story. He published "Sakurajima" in 1946, and *Hino Hate* ("End of the Sun") in 1947, establishing himself as one of the major postwar writers. His novel *Nise no Kisetsu* ("Season of Forgery") is a portrait of a nihilist, while *Suna Dokei* ("Hourglass") is a satire on a morally devastated society. He won the Shinchō Award for the latter work in 1954 and the Naoki Prize for his *Boroya no Shunjū* ("Shanty Life") the same year. *Genka* ("Illusion") followed eleven years later, and he died in 1965.

Tamiki Hara

Summer Flower

I WENT DOWNTOWN AND bought some flowers, thinking I would visit the grave of my wife. In my pocket I had a bundle of incense sticks that I had taken from the Buddhist altar in my home. Wednesday would be the first anniversary for the soul of my wife, but it was doubtful whether my native town would survive until then. Although most factories were closed that day due to electric power rationing, there was no one to be seen except myself–walking along the street with flowers, in the early morning. I did not know the name of the flowers, but they looked like a summer variety with the rustic beauty of their tiny yellow petals.

As I sprayed water over the gravestone exposed to the scorching heat of the sun, divided the flowers into two bunches and put them in the vases on either side, the grave appeared rather refreshing, and I gazed at the flowers and the stone for awhile. Underneath the grave were buried not only the ashes of my wife but also those of my parents. After burning the incense sticks that I had brought and making a bow, I drank out of the well beside the grave. Then I went home by way of Nigitsu Park. The scent of the incense remained in my pocket throughout that day and the next. It was on the third day after my visit to the grave that the bomb was dropped.

My life was saved because I was in the bathroom. On

the morning of August 6, I had gotten up around eight o'clock. The air-raid alarm had sounded twice the night before and nothing had happened, so that before dawn I had taken off my clothes and slept in my night robe, which I had not put on for a long time. Such being the case, I had on only my shorts when I got up. My younger sister, when she saw me, complained of my rising late, but I went into the bathroom without replying.

I do not remember how many seconds passed after that. All of a sudden, a powerful blow struck me and darkness fell before my eyes. Involuntarily I shouted and held my hands over my head. Aside from the sound of something like the crashing of a storm, I could not tell what it was in the complete darkness. I groped for the door, opened it, and found the veranda. Until then, I had been hearing my own voice exclaiming, "Wah!" amid the rushing sounds, agonized at not being able to see. But after I came out to the veranda, the scene of destruction gradually loomed in the dusk before my eyes and I became clearly conscious.

It looked like an episode from a loathsome dream. At first, when the blow struck my head, and I lost my sight, I knew that I had not been killed. Then I became angry, thinking that things had become very troublesome. And my own shouts sounded almost like the voice of somebody else. But when I could see, vaguely as it was, the things around me, I felt as if I were standing stage center in a tragic play. Certainly I had beheld such a scene in a movie. Beyond the clouds of dust, patches of blue sky began to come into view. Light came in through holes in the walls and from other unexpected directions. As I walked gingerly on the boards where the tatami flooring had been blown off, my younger sister came rushing toward me. "You weren't hurt? You weren't hurt? Are you all right? Your eyes are bleeding. Go wash right away." She told me that there was still water running in the kitchen scullery.

Finding myself completely naked, I turned to my younger sister and asked her, "Can you at least get me something to put on?" She was able to pull out a pair of shorts from the closet that had been saved from destruction. Someone rushed in with a bewildered gesture. His face was smeared in blood. He wore only a shirt. This man was an employee of a nearby factory. Seeing me, he said, "It's lucky you were saved." Then he bustled away, muttering, "Telephone....I have to make a telephone call."

There were crevices everywhere, and the doors, screens, and tatami mats were scattered about. The pillars and doorsills were clearly exposed, and the whole building was filled with a strange silence. Later I was told that most houses were completely destroyed in that area, but my second floor did not give way; even the floor boards remained firm. My father, a painstaking builder, had built our house about forty years before, and it had been solidly constructed.

Tramping about over the littered mats and screens, I looked among scattered articles for something to wear. The book which I had left half read the night before was there on the floor with its pages turned up. The picture frame which had fallen from the beam overhead stood tinged with death in front of the *tokonoma*. I found my canteen quite unexpectedly, and then my hat. Still unable to find my pants, I started looking for something else to cover myself.

K of the factory office appeared on the veranda of the drawing room. Seeing me, he cried in a sad voice, "I'm hurt! Help me!" and dropped down in a heap where he stood. Blood was oozing from his forehead, and his eyes were glistening with tears.

"Where is it?" I asked, and he distorted his pale wrinkled face, saying, "My knees," as he held them with his hand. I gave him a strip of cloth, and I drew over my own legs two pairs of socks, one over the other.

"It's started to smoke. Let's get out of here. Help me get away." K, who was considerably older than I but usually much more vigorous, seemed to be highly disturbed.

Looking out from the veranda, I could see nothing recognizable except the clusters of flattened houses and a ferro-concrete building a little farther away. Beside the toppled-over mud wall there was a tall maple tree whose trunk was torn off halfway up; the twigs had been thrown into the wash basin. Suddenly K stopped by the air-raid shelter, and said, "Why don't we stay here? There's a water tank, besides. . . ." When I said, "No, let's go to the river," he asked me wonderingly, "The river? Which direction is the river?"

I took a night robe out of the closet, handed it to him, and tore the shelter curtain. I picked up a cushion, too. When I turned the mat on the veranda, I found my emergency bag. I felt relieved and put the bag on my shoulder. Small red flames rose from the warehouse of the chemical factory next door. We went out over the completely twisted maple.

That tall tree had stood in the corner of the garden for a long time, and had been an object of dreamy imagination in my childhood. Recently I had come back and started living at my own home after a long time, and now I thought it odd that even this tree did not evoke the same old sweet memory. What was strange was that my home town itself had lost its soft natural atmosphere, and I felt it to be something like a composition of cruel, inorganic matter. Every time I went into the drawing room facing the garden, the title, *The Fall of the House of Usher*, spontaneously sprang to my mind.

K and I climbed over the crumbling houses, clearing obstacles from our path, and walked slowly at first. We came to level ground, and knew that we were on the road, where we walked faster down the middle. Suddenly there called a voice from behind a crushed building, crying, "Please!" Turning back, I found that the voice belonged to a woman with a blood-stained face walking toward us. "Help me!" she cried, following us desperately. We had walked on for some time when we passed an old woman who stood in the middle of the path with her legs wide apart. She was crying like a child, "The house is catching fire! The house is catching fire!" Smoke rose here and there from the crumbling houses, and suddenly we came upon a spot where breaths of flame belched furiously.

We passed it running. The road became level again, and we found ourselves at the foot of Sakae Bridge. Here the refugees gathered one after another. Someone who had stationed himself on the bridge cried out: "Those who are strong enough, put out the fire!" I walked toward the grove of Asana Park, and there became separated from K.

The bamboo grove had been mowed down, and a path made through the grove under the tramping feet of refugees. Most of the trees overhead had been torn apart in midair, and this famous old garden on the river was now disfigured with pockmarks and gashes. Beside a hedge was a middle-aged woman, her ample body slumped over limply. Even as I looked, something infectious seemed to emanate from her lifeless face. It was the first such face I had seen. But I was to see many, many more that were more grotesque.

In the grove facing the riverbank I came across a group of students. These girls had escaped from a factory, and all had been injured slightly, but now, trembling from the freshness of the thing that had happened before their very eyes, they chattered excitedly. At that moment my eldest brother appeared. He wore only a shirt, but looked unhurt. He had a beer bottle in one hand. The houses on the other bank of the river had collapsed and were on fire, but the electric poles still stood. Sitting on the narrow road by the riverbank, I felt I was all right now. What had been threatening me, what had been destined to happen, had taken place at last. I could consider myself as one who survived. I have to keep a record of this, I said to myself. But I scarcely knew the truth about the air raid then.

The fire on the opposite bank of the river raged more furiously. The scorching heat reached this side of the river, so that we had to dip the cushion in the rising river water and put it over our heads. Then someone shouted, "Air raid!" and all the people crawled into the heart of the grove.

The sun sent forth its bright rays, and the other side of the grove seemed to be on fire. A hot wind blew overhead, and black smoke was fanned up toward the middle of the river. Then the sky suddenly grew dark, and large drops came down in torrents. The rain reduced the heat momentarily, but soon the sky cleared up again.

I walked along a stone embankment down to the water's edge and discovered a large wooden box floating along at my feet, and around it bobbed onions that had spilled out. Pulling the box to me, I took out the onions and handed them to people on the bank. The box had been thrown out of a freight train which had been overturned on the bridge upstream. While I was picking up the onions, there came a voice crying, "Help!" Clinging to a piece of wood, a young girl drifted in the middle of the river, floating at one time and sinking at another. I took a large timber and swam toward her pushing it. Although I had not swum for a long time, I managed to help her more easily than I had expected.

The fire on the opposite bank, which had slackened for a while, had started raging again. This time, murky smoke mingled with the red flames, and as the roiling mass expanded, the heat of the flames seemed to grow more intense with each second. When the fire finally burned itself out, there remained only an empty carcass. It was then that I sensed a wall of air undulating towards us over the water. Tornado! Even as the thought struck me, a blast of wind passed over our heads. The grass and trees around me trembled, and whole trees were plucked out and snatched high into the air.

When the tornado had passed, the sky showed that evening was near. My second elder brother appeared quite unexpectedly. His shirt was torn in back, and there was a brushing trace the color of thin India ink on his face which later became a suppurating burn. Coming home on business, he had sighted a small airplane in the sky and then three strange flashes. After being thrown on the ground, he had run to rescue his wife and the maid-servant, who were struggling under the collapsed house. He entrusted his two children to the maid and let them escape before him, and then spent much time in saving the old man who lived next door.

My brother and I walked upstream still looking for a ferryboat. The sinking sun made everything around us look pale, and both on and beneath the bank there were pale people who cast their shadows on the water. When we passed before them, these people spoke to us in faint, gentle voices, "Give us some water."

Someone called me in a sharp, pitiful voice. Below I saw a naked young boy whose lifeless body was completely buried in the water, and two women squatting on the stone steps less than four feet from the corpse. Their faces were swollen twice their natural size, distorted in an ugly way, and only their scorched rumpled hair showed that they were women. Looking at them, I shuddered rather than felt pity.

We found a little raft, untied the rope, and rowed toward the opposite bank of the river. Daylight had already turned dusky when the raft reached the sand beach on the other side, and the area was scattered with wounded townsmen. A soldier who was squatting by the river said to me, "Let me drink some hot water." I had him lean against my shoulder and we walked together. As he staggered on the sand, the soldier muttered, "It's much better to be killed." I made him wait beside the path.

Nearing a water-supply station I beheld the large burned head of a human being slowly drinking hot water out of a cup; the enormous face seemed to be made up of black soybeans; and the hair above the ears was burned off in a straight line where the man's cap had not protected it. I filled a cup and took it to the soldier.

People were starting to cook their supper, burning pieces of wood on the sandy beach. As the tide began to rise, we all moved up the bank. Night had fallen, and a breeze sprang up. It was too cool for us to sleep, and we kept hearing voices here and there crying desperately for water.

Nigitsu Park was nearby but it was now wrapped in darkness, and we could see only faintly the broken trees. My brother lay in a hollow in the ground and I placed myself in another shallow place. Close to me lay three or four wounded schoolgirls. "The grove over there has started burning," someone said. "Don't you think we'd better move away from here?" Getting out of the hollow, I saw flame glaring over the top of the trees ahead of us, but there was no sign of the fire spreading up to our spot.

There must still have been an undamaged siren somewhere, for we heard its warning faint in the distance.

"I wish morning would come!" a wounded girl complained.

From the direction of the riverbed came death cries, in a young voice still strong. "Water! Water! Please....! Mother....Sister....Mitchan....! The agonized words, interspersed with moans and weak gasps of pain, seemed to wrench his whole body.

A dispensary had been established near the entrance to the Toshogu Shrine. With each case a policeman formally asked the patient his permanent address and age; and the patient, even after receiving a slip of paper identifying him, still had to wait about an hour in a long row, under the scorching sun. Patients who were able to join that row were more fortunate than the rest. Now someone cried furiously, "Soldier! Soldier! Help me! Soldier!" A horribly burned young girl rolled in anguish on the roadside. And near her was a man in the uniform of an air-defense guard, who complained in feeble voice, "Please help me, ah, Nurse, Doctor!" as he laid his head, swollen and bloated with burns, on a stone, and opened his blackened mouth. No one gave heed to him. Policemen, doctors, and nurses came from other towns to help, but they were rather few in number.

Under a cherry tree two school-girls lay groaning for water, faces burned black, their thin shoulders exposed to the scorching sun. They were students of the girls' commercial school who had met the disaster while potato

digging in the vicinity. A woman whose face had been smoke-dried joined them. Placing her handbag on the ground, she stretched out her legs listlessly, oblivious to the dying girls.

The second night dragged by. Before dawn some unknown voice took up a Buddhist invocation, a sound suggesting that people were dying all the time. The two commercial students died when the morning sun was high. A policeman, when he had finished examining the girls' bodies lying face down in the ditch, approached the dead woman nearby. He opened her handbag and found a savings passbook and public loan bonds in it. She still wore the traveling suit in which she had been struck.

About noon, the air-raid warning sounded again and the roar of planes was heard. Although I had become used to the ugliness and misery around me, my fatigue and hunger became more and more intense. People died one after another, and their bodies were left as they were. Men walked restlessly, without hope of assistance.

The desperate clarion call of the bugle came from the parade ground, and at the same moment my eldest brother appeared. He had stopped the previous day at Hatsukaichi, which his sister-in-law had evacuated, and had hired a wagon. Together we decided to leave the place, and so we searched out my second elder brother's family and my sister and set off past the entrance of Asano Garden.

My second elder brother caught sight of a body in the vacant lot toward the West Parade Ground. It was clothed in yellow pants that were familiar to us. It was Fumihiko, my nephew. Fluid flowed from a swelling on his breast the size of a fist. His white teeth were dimly visible in his blackened face, and the fingers of both hands were bent inward with the nails boring into the skin. Beside him sprawled the body of a schoolboy and that of a young woman. They lay slightly apart. Both had become rigid in their last positions. My second elder brother stripped off Fumihiko's nails and his belt for a keepsake. Placing a name card on him, we left the spot.

The wagon then passed Kokutaiji Temple and Sumiyoshi Bridge, and came to Koi, giving me an almost full view of the burned sites of the busiest quarters. Amid the vast, silvery expanse of nothingness that lay under the glaring sun, there were the roads, the river, the bridges, and the stark naked, swollen bodies. The limbs of these corpses, which seemed to have become rigid after struggling in their last agony, had a kind of haunting rhythm. In the scattered electric wires and countless wrecks there was embodied a spasmodic design in nothingness. The burnt and toppled streetcar and the horse with its huge belly on the ground gave me the impression of a world described by a Dali surrealist painting. The tall camphor tree in the precincts of Kokutaiji Temple had been felled completely, and the gravestones too were scattered. The Asana Library, with only its outer block left, had been turned into a morgue. The roads were still smoky here and there and were permeated with a cadaverous smell. Somehow it seems that impressions of the scene are more aptly put in *katakana*:*

The strange rhythm of the human bodies,
  inflamed and red,
That mingle with the glaring wrecks
  and the cinders of grayish white
In the vast panorama—
Is this all that has happened, or is it
  what could have happened?
Oh, the world stripped of all in an
  instant.
How the swollen belly of the horse
  glares beside the toppled streetcar.
And the stench of the smoldering wires!

The wagon proceeded along the endless road through the debris. Even on the outskirts of the city, the houses all had collapsed, and it was only after we had passed

* *Katakana* letters or signs are much simpler and starker in appearance than the other forms used in writing Japanese.

Kusatsu that we were at last liberated from the shadow of disaster and were greeted by the sight of living green. The appearance of the dragonflies that flitted so swiftly above the emerald rice paddies was touchingly refreshing to my eyes. From here stretched a long, monotonous road to Yawata Village. Night had fallen by the time we reached there, and all was dismally quiet.

The next day, our miserable life—of the aftermath—truly began. The wounded did not recover satisfactorily, and even those who at first had been strong gradually grew weak from lack of food. Our maid's arm suppurated badly, and flies gathered around the burned part, which finally became infested with maggots. No matter how often we sterilized the area, the maggots never ceased to infest the wound. She died a little more than a month later.

Four or five days after we had moved to the village, my nephew, who had been last seen on his way to school, suddenly reappeared. On the morning that he had gone to his school—his building later was to be evacuated—he had seen the flash from inside his classroom. In an instant he hid himself under the desk, and was buried under the falling ceiling, but crawled out through a crevice. There were only four or five boys who had escaped—the rest were killed by the first blow. The survivors ran toward Hiji Hill, and he vomited white fluid on the way. Then he went to the home of one of his friends with whom he had escaped, and there he was sheltered. About a week after his return, my nephew's hair began to fall out, and his nose bled. His doctor declared that his condition was already critical, but my nephew gradually gained his strength again.

My friend N suffered a different experience. He was on his way to visit an evacuated factory, and his train had just entered a tunnel. As the train came out, he saw three parachutes floating down through the air over Hiroshima several miles behind. Arriving at the next station, he was surprised to find that the window glasses were broken. By the time he reached his destination, detailed information already had been circulated. He took the first train back to Hiroshima. Every train that passed was filled with people grotesquely wounded. When he arrived at the town, he could not wait until the fire was quenched, and so he proceeded along the still hot asphalt road.

He went first to the girls' high school where his wife was teaching. On the site of the classrooms lay the bones of the pupils, and on the site of the principal's office lay bones that seemed to have belonged to the principal. Nothing could he identify as the remains of his wife. He hurried back to his own home. Being near Ujina, the house had crumbled without burning. Yet he could not find his wife there either. Then he examined all the bodies lying on the road that led from his home to the girls' school. Most of the bodies were lying on their faces, so that he had to turn them over with his hands in order to examine them. Every woman had been changed miserably, but his wife's body was not there. Finally he wandered around without direction. He saw some ten bodies heaped in a pile in a cistern.

Then there were three bodies that had become rigid as they held a ladder set against the riverbank, and others stood waiting in a row for the bus, the nails of each fastening against the shoulders of the one ahead. The terrible scene of the West Parade Ground was beyond description. There were piles of soldier corpses all around —but the body of his wife was not to be found anywhere.

My friend N visited all the barracks, and looked into the faces of the severely wounded people. Every face was miserable beyond words, but none of the faces was his wife's. After looking for three days and nights at so many charred bodies, dead and living, N at last went back to the burned site of his wife's school.

Translated by George Saito

Tamiki Hara was born in Hiroshima in 1905. He graduated from Keio University, majoring in English literature. He published short stories and poems in college literary society magazines after graduating and was greatly influenced by Dadaism and Marxism in the early 1930's. He published a collection of short stories and poems, but was not given great recognition as a writer. He experienced the atomic bomb in Hiroshima in 1945, after which his style greatly changed. "Summer Flower" was written in 1947. He describes the catastrophe rather calmly, but the sincere lament and prayer expressed in his story won great acclaim. He was awarded the first Minakami Takitarō Prize for his work. He continued to write novels and poems based on his experience of the atomic bomb. He committed suicide after finishing *Shingan no Kuni* ("The Land of One's Desire") in 1951.

Fumiko Hayashi

Bones

"And why beholdest thou the mote that is in thy brother's eye, but considerest not the beam that is in thine own eye?" (Matthew 7, iii)

"PLEASE RETURN THE BONES to me."

Michiko thought it was quite strange. What would the government minister's wife do with the bones, once they were hers? She shut her eyes tight, and hot tears began to form at the corners. Perhaps her present attitude proved that she had really turned into a heartless monster. But hadn't her own life changed completely ever since her husband's empty bone box came back? Surprisingly enough, no one actually seemed to care when she told them her story. And after reading in the paper that a former government minister's wife had petitioned to have her husband's bones returned, following his execution at the gallows as a war criminal, she suddenly wanted to burst into tears.

On cold rainy nights, Michiko picked up men on the streets.

"One. . . . two. . . . three. . . ." she counted, as she held her breath and gazed steadily toward the station. When someone approached her, she wanted to cry out, "Wait! Give me some bones!"

From time to time, men thin as ghosts shuffled out of the station. Their bones creaked as they made their way in her direction. Their lonely, glimmering eyes approached her, shining brightly.

What happened on the first day was repeated over and over again. For Michiko that initial experience was unforgettable.

"How much?" the man asked.

She became flustered and giggled several times as she pressed the back of her hand to her lips. Finally, when she realized that it meant the price of spending the night with her, the region around her waist began to turn numb. She walked with the man as if in a daze. There was a smell of medicine about him. She went to the hotel which the more experienced Ran-chan had shown her.

In the few minutes which elapsed while they passed by the Musashino Theater, where the waitresses from the nearby cafes were hunting for customers, and arrived in front of the tiny shack of the Moulin Rouge Playhouse, she gradually gained courage. Could it be that the thin crescent moon above the cliff directly in front of them was causing the tremor of excitement in her? She walked between the parched illumination of the neon lights on both sides of the road, at times stumbling on the bumpy pavement. In her mind, she secretly clasped her hands in prayer toward the indifferent moon.

The smell of medicine lingered. "He must be a doctor," she thought. So far, they had had no opportunity to observe each other closely.

As he drew nearer, the touch of his overcoat caused a prickly sensation on the back of her hand. The wind, which swooped down from the cliff, had a fishy smell as if they were on a large lake. Michiko became aware of various sounds. . . . In the darkness, the ground shook below the rocky ridge. The passing trains creaked like glass boxes.

"Aren't we there yet?" he asked.

"No," she replied.

"Is it a hotel?"

"Yes."

For no apparent reason, the man stopped short and looked back. Whenever anyone approached them, he drew apart and walked ahead of her, his hat drawn over his face.

She shuddered at this behavior but walked leisurely—at a distance from him. From the back, he had a shabby appearance.

The dark, stone cliff resembled a pile of rags.

She turned sharply and climbed up the crooked, uneven stone steps. Having realized his mistake, the man quickly retraced his steps and ran up the stairs behind her, panting heavily.

When they reached the Ome Highway, the moon faced them directly, shining high above the sea of neon lights below. She could see the tracks of the Keio Line, corrugated like the keys of a xylophone. The trains stirred up storms of dust as they passed. Their ominous roar, rushing toward them in waves, reverberated like the beckoning call of death from the underworld.

Her companion relaxed and came closer. "Tell me frankly," he said, "how much do you want?"

Michiko shyly concealed her nose with the shawl and answered, "I don't know. This is my first time."

"Really? This is your first time?....You're a liar!"

The region around her breasts suddenly became flushed and she gently wiped her nose with the velvet shawl.

"You seem like a nice girl," he said in a conciliatory tone.

Twice, she sneezed lightly and blew her nose with the corner of the shawl.

In the dusky sky there were long, thin layers of frothy clouds. Crossing the wide road, they descended again to the bottom of a dark cliff and headed toward the shanty town in Hinode-cho. When they finally came in front of the Kekkoya, the hotel she had visited on the previous day, a baby buggy was parked next to the wall, and a woman with a white apron stood by, looking uncomfortably cold.

The maid whom she had met yesterday was alert and led them to a dark room at the back of the second floor. The wooden floorboards, which were full of knotholes, squeaked noisily as they walked through.

Wallpaper decorated with chrysanthemums hung limply on the sliding door.

The maid immediately called her out in the hall and asked, "Say, did you get paid?"

"No, not yet," Michiko said.

"You should get it first. Ran-chan is already here. Are you going to stay for the night?"

"I don't know."

"Then, get him to stay here and have him order something to drink. You'll be all right. I'll leave the bedding out in the hall. Anyway, get what's due and find out whether he's staying overnight. You've got to pay the cashier."

"Yes."

Michiko wrapped the dingy shawl tightly around herself and went inside. The man was standing with his gray hat propped on the back of his head. He was younger than she had expected. And contrary to her previous impression, once inside he seemed to be much taller. It must have been the low ceiling. He was thin. He looked at the wristwatch on his bony wrist.

"Shall we stay for the night?" he asked.

Michiko was relieved. She cupped her mouth with her hand and gave a wan smile. The man appeared to be particularly pleased with himself and took her hand; the touch of his warm, moist hands made her feel wretched.

"I'll have to take the money to the cashier," she said.

He seemed to understand her plight and, squatting down on the rough straw mat, he took out an old, worn wallet.

"How much?" he asked.

Michiko frowned. Although Ran-chan had told her to get as much as possible, somehow she could not talk about such things. She heard the bedding being placed out in the hall; the sliding door at the entrance bulged inward. The man counted ten 100-yen bills and put them in her hand.

"By the way, would you like something to drink?" she asked.

"I'll just have two bottles of saké and some peanuts."

She went out into the hallway, stepping over the bedding,

and walked downstairs to the cashier. The latter took six of the bills from her.

On the way back, when she went to the toilet, a tall girl with only a slip on and a coat draped over her shoulder shook loose her hair as she ran out of the water closet. Slamming the toilet door shut with a bang, she passed Michiko and pattered down the hall.

The interior of the water closet smelled of fresh, flower-shaped, pink napthalene. This scent mingled with the traces of the offensive perfume the girl must have worn.

Michiko took the hundred-yen bills out of her purse and counted four. She was about to cry. Opening the small window in the toilet she breathed in the cold air. In that brief moment, all her memories of the past seemed to rush back in a mighty torrent. The reflection of headlights lit the window glass brightly and abruptly faded away.... There must be a highway below. She put both arms on the dirty window sill and propped her chin, weeping bitterly as she inhaled the freezing air.

She tried to think about her dead husband. She reflected that her present situation was unavoidable.

"There must be some other way...," he seemed to be whispering in her ear.

Michiko answered that there might have been, but she no longer had the strength to look for one. The faces of her father, Emiko, and Kanji spun in front of her like picture cards. Having cried herself out, she felt much better. She took out her compact and pressed the grimy powerpuff firmly around her reddened eyes.

When she went upstairs, the man and the maid were speaking to each other in low whispers. He was pouring the saké by himself into the cup on the tray. Scooping up three or four 100-yen bills, the maid brushed by Michiko on the way out.

"How about a drink?" the man said.

"I don't drink," she replied.

The bedding was piled in one corner. The scroll picture

on the wall of a beautiful girl was probably a printed copy. The slender beauty stood with a hand in her hair. From the ruffled hem of her garment a slim leg extended from the vermilion underskirt.

There was a single window. The thin green walls would allow everything from the other side to be heard. In the small, four-and-a-half mat room, a partially burned out mosquito coil remained on the window ledge.

"This is terrible saké," he said.

"Oh?" she responded.

"They probably make money by mixing it with water."

"Is that so?"

"How old are you?"

"Much older than you think."

"Let me guess."

"All right."

"Are you twenty-five?"

"No, twenty-six."

"You don't look your age."

"Don't you think so?"

"Are you a widow?"

"No. . . ."

"Don't tell me you've never slept with a man before."

"Well. . . . actually I was married once."

"Did he die in the war?"

"Yes."

The man finished one bottle and began on the second.

Suddenly from the adjoining room, she clearly heard the harsh voice of a woman cry out, "Now, stop that! You're tickling me!"

Holding the bottle in his hand, the man raised his head without a smile. Its absence made his expression seem frightening. His long chin reminded her of an old advertisement for Kao Toilet Soap. Michiko could not quite make up her mind about spending the night with him and kept stalling nervously, fidgeting with the worn metal clasp of her handbag.

All of a sudden, she thought of the woman in the white

apron standing near the baby buggy when they came in. How strange that she should be reminded of her now. It was absurd. The woman had a blank expression. Perhaps the face was particularly hazy because her attention had been drawn to the white apron in the darkness. Also, this scene may have made a deep impression since the buggy was quite similar to the one which she once used for her daughter, Emiko. Michiko had a strange premonition that this scene would return to haunt her in the future. Something struck against the other side of the wall. With her head bent, Michiko traced random words on her knee with her finger. She could not hold back this growing, oppressive feeling that her whole body was turning into ice, that the deep torment within her soul would overflow, and seep out through her fingertips as tears of anguish. It would take stubborn courage to last out this night. A deep, murky sigh began to form in her throat.

"How did you find a place like this?" the man asked.

"A friend of mine told me," she answered.

The man merely grunted a reply, apparently not interested in prying into her personal affairs.

Being petite, Michiko's knees were tiny, and when she sat down, she looked more like a schoolgirl. But her breasts rose fully against the shapeless, navy blue coat and the frayed jacket of a faded cream color. She had a slender neck and a small face.

"How did you get that sore on your neck?"

"Well, when I was a little girl, I had lymphangitus and had it operated on."

There was an inch-long scar swelling on her thin neck.

"Are you a doctor?" she asked.

The man gave a wide grin and showed his unsightly teeth for the first time.

"Do I look like one?" he replied.

"Yes," she said.

The man remained evasive on this point. He did not even carry a valise and seemed to be leading a comfortable existence. After drinking the saké, he yawned slightly, took out a package of *Peace* from his coat pocket, and lit one with a lighter.

"We'd better get ready for bed," he suggested.

"What time is it?" she asked.

"A little past ten."

It was a curt, impersonal reply, which gave her no chance to make a friendly overture.

When she began clumsily to lay out the bedding, he stood up and went to the toilet. She spread out the poorly starched sheeting and put the two thin quilts on top. The green rayon stitches on the quilts were unraveling in places, and the cotton filling was coming out. When the man returned, he opened the sliding door wide.

"Isn't it cold?" he asked.

"It's because there are no curtains on the walls," she explained.

Without any display of emotion, he quickly took off his coat and trousers, and practically wrenched off the tie, then removed his gray sweater and white shirt. When he was down to his knitted brown underwear, he slid between the covers.

"Damn, it's cold! Say, put all my things on top of the bed," he said, as he raised his head and pointed with his chin, "and while you're at it, lock the door."

"Yes."

Michiko placed a glass ashtray by his pillow. The cigarette which he had started to smoke had gone out, retaining most of its original length. After she had attended to the flimsy lock and carefully laid out his carelessly strewn clothes on the reclining figure, the edge of the quilt began to twitch nervously. What appeared to be crumpled long underwear and briefs peeked out.

Her heart suddenly stopped beating, and she was overcome by a feeling of utter disgust.

She recalled a poem by Storm, which she had read as a school girl: "Today, only today. . . ." She had forgotten the next line but remembered the rest well:

"Tomorrow, alas, tomorrow–
Everything must pass away.
Only this hour,
You are mine.
To die, alas, to die–
I die alone."

Michiko liked it so much that she had sent it in a letter to her husband who was then overseas. She had even written: "If you should die, my daughter and I will commit suicide and follow you." Every time she heard the words, "The Potsdam Declaration," she thought of Storm's biography where it mentioned that he had left his brithplace in Husum, gone to Potsdam, and become an assistant judge at a military court. She was perfectly certain that Potsdam was the place where Storm had lived. She had no special interest in literature herself, but had friends in school who did, and among the books she was persuaded to read, Michiko had come across this poem by the German poet, which had particularly appealed to her.

She ignored the articles of underwear protruding from the quilt, as if they were unfit to be touched.

"God, it's cold. Come on in and get warm!"

After extending this invitation, the man deliberately chattered his teeth.

She took off her overcoat and stockings and turned off the light. In the total darkness, the cold suddenly penetrated her whole body. It was not entirely from the cold alone, but Michiko began to tremble.

The man repeated, "Hey, hurry up and get in!"

Michiko remained sleepless all night. She saw the night turning slowly into dawn. The man slept soundly on his stomach, snoring. The stains on the ceiling gradually became visible. It was perfectly still within the four walls. The man's rough legs began to annoy her; they had slept back to back because it was so cold. She searched for her underskirt with her feet, drew it closer, and thrust both feet in while still remaining in bed.

"Ah!" a sigh escaped from her throat. She could not help feeling terribly guilty. Staring blankly at the frosted glass which had brightened to blue-green, she felt like asking some god if this was human fate.

The man turned over, felt his way with his hand, and encircled one arm around her waist, over the jacket she was wearing. A soul, which had been confined to isolation, began to flutter its wings more freely than the night before. She gently entwined her hand in his arm. She thought how comforting it was to have someone beside her. True, she felt no particular fondness for him, but even in this short period, Michiko and become used to him. His arm remained unresponsive.

All at once she saw the baby buggy and the woman standing, her white apron blown by the cold wind.

Long ago, she had spent a similar hour with her husband. She felt such remorse that it seemed to set her ears ringing.

With her right hand, Michiko wiped the tears which were falling on the pillow. With the other, she softly caressed his big-boned arm. She concluded that it was rather simple to degrade oneself and felt the burden lighten on her shoulder.

Nearby, a rooster was announcing daybreak.

The man made a whistling sound as he moaned, apparently having a nightmare. Michiko gazed at the wall with her eyes wide open. The sound reminded her of someone being buried alive.

She felt as though she were asleep, carrying a very sick patient on her back, and did not feel at all degraded. Man must have been created as a cruel animal. Michiko tried to tell herself that it was all her fault. She had tried to stake her entire future on the single fact of being resolutely faithful to her husband–so, when he was killed, she had deservingly fallen into her present predicament. Naturally, she was quite aware of the seriousness of her offence, although she tried to convince herself that she had merely allowed the use of her body for a price.

The sparkling of water cast a brilliant reflection on the window glass. It appeared to be raining.

The man woke up, aroused by his own cries. "Oh, I had a terrible dream," he said. His hair, touching the nape of her neck, felt cold.

"What kind of a dream was it?" she asked.

"Well, I killed a soldier. I killed a dying man. . . . fried his flesh and ate it. . . ."

"That's horrible. Were you fighting overseas?"

"Yes, six years."

"Did you kill anybody?"

"No, never. . . . But I did kill a snake in the mountains near Manila and ate it. I was on the verge of dying, though. . . . . Where did your man get killed?"

As she answered, "Okinawa," the recollection became a burden; only the present moment pushed steadily forward.

When daylight came, the sky was overcast, and it was raining.

Like two people exiled on a lonely island, they sometimes took turns raising their heads to look through the visible portion of the window, just to pass the time away.

Their souls, which had been totally shattered, were shimmering like countless fish scales, each aglow with its own fragmentary memory. Having experienced the war together, they shared something in common and remained mutually silent as if they had just come off the operating table. The same feeling of lassitude, which suppressed any desire to recall the past through the chaos of the war, simply let them lie there.

The man stood up, put on his coat, and went to the toilet. Michiko took out her compact and dabbled the powderpuff on her dry forehead and cheeks. The sound of the rain-water rushing through the drains became louder.

She tried to guess what he did for a living. Quietly extending her arm, she inserted one hand into the pockets of the coat lying on top of the bed. She felt a worn wallet, a name-card case, a pipe, and what seemed to be a stack of hundred-yen bills, folded into two, amounting to four or five thousand yen. Hearing a noise in the hallway, she quickly threw the coat back to its original place, and withdrew her hands back into bed.

"Oh, it's cold!"

The man tucked in his chin, got back into bed, and crawled on his belly to pull over the ashtray. He looked at the wristwatch beside the pillow and said, "I guess it's time to get up."

"Are you going to work now?" she asked.

"Do I look like it?" he replied.

While he lit a cigarette and inhaled deeply, one of his hands reached for her stomach. Overcome with a strange excitement, she tried to imagine its final goal. She thought: "If this moment would only last a day or two. . . ."

As the night turned into day, the four walls, by contrast, seemed to grow darker.

The alarm clock rang insistently downstairs.

With an ambivalent feeling, by no means devoid of affection, Michiko drew closer to him. . . . There was no past or future. . . . Her cries of rapture were muted by the sound of the falling rain. . . . She began to embrace the man in front of her with fierce desperation. On a sudden vindictive impulse she bit into his fingernail.

Michiko never saw him again. In the meantime, she plunged directly into the life of a prostitute. Little by little, she became accustomed to her work, and as experience increased, she no longer felt the intense passion of that first night. Successively, she accommodated herself to the depravity of men.

Perhaps it was because all her partners were attracted to her by physical necessity, but they all seemed to have just one thing on their minds. All the simple men, requiring no explanation, milled around her. Michiko had a small face with a narrow forehead, and her front teeth protruded slightly. The men regarded her habit of concealing her teeth as a mark of inexperience.

When night came, she became alive. She could choose her own partner. She carefully set her sight on each man who approached her and even learned to guess the worth of a wallet at a glance.

The harsh wind buffeting her cheeks stimulated one notion: it was pride in the recognition that her existence was important and necessary. And she could hardly wait for night to arrive. She also acquired a knack for finding different places to sleep.

Michiko contracted venereal disease, but the medical students whom she knew gave her penicillin, at cost. Three of them shared an upstairs room, and she received her painful shots, lying on their dirty bedding. When they gave her a thorough physical examination, she was mindful to act coquettishly like a young girl, realizing its effect on the young men.

She had tuberculosis.

For Michiko and her husband it had been a love marriage. But now those sweet memories had less substance than a dream, all having vanished like bubbles into the distant past. She only caught glimpses of her dead husband's image in the face of her daughter.

Since the March 9th air raid on downtown Tokyo when her house in Ishihara-cho was destroyed, Michiko had already moved six times, and now rented a room on the second floor of a laundry at Araki-cho in the Yotsuya district. Her father had once been an army colonel. He had retired twenty years before and drew a pension, working for an insurance company at the same time. Her mother had died in the same year that she finished girls' school, and upon graduation, Michiko began to work for an insurance company in the Marunouchi district, a job arranged through an introduction by her father's acquaintance.

She had met her husband in the same section where she was working, and they were married without a wedding ceremony, keeping the affair a secret at the office for almost a year. Soon after their marriage, the Pacific war began. At the end of 1943, her husband was sent overseas. He had an older brother in Nagasaki, also a naval officer, who was already in the fighting. The daughter was born just before he left for overseas, and Michiko had the baby's name recorded in the official register. But the modest, peaceful existence lasted only briefly. About the same time as her husband's death on Okinawa, her father became crippled with rheumatism. The war ended shortly thereafter.

Her younger brother, Kanji, came back from a factory in Kawasaki where he had been a student-worker. However, he had developed tuberculosis while on the job and remained idle. And after he had spewed blood at the bathhouse and was carried home on a stretcher, he remained bedridden. It was an impossible situation. The father's pension was cut off, and he was no longer able to work at the office due to his illness.

Since Michiko could speak a little English, she found a job with the American Red Cross, but suffering from a lung ailment, she could not keep it up for more than six months. She tried knitting as a sideline and worked as a canvasser for a dress shop. Because she was physically frail, these jobs did not work out too well, either. One day quite by chance, Michiko met Aizawa Ranko. They had both held similar jobs at the insurance company. The latter dropped in frequently after that to urge her to become a prostitute–an easily acquired profession. She mulled over this possibility for several months.

Ranko would say, "Even if you behave rather scandalously, no one will be the wiser or even bother to look back. You'll all starve while you're trying to make up your mind."

When she was spoken to in this way, Michiko was almost persuaded. Still, when she saw her brother's hollow eyes or watched her father's crawling figure, she did not have

the heart to degrade herself. Nevertheless, when she saw her own daughter, Emiko, whom she loved so much, innocently playing–putting flowers into the empty bone box –she could not help but waver. It was a simple container with a bit of red earth on the bottom. Emiko placed the flowers in this box and asked, "They're for Daddy, aren't they?"

Michiko made up her mind and sought Ranko's advice.

According to the doctor, Kanji would not live to see the New Year. She was tired of nursing his lingering illness. At times, she even prayed for his early demise. He must have sensed his sister's attitude. Usually, he remained silent all day, but on rare occasions when something upset him, a scene would occur, as when Kanji grabbed the water glass beside his pillow with his skinny hand and flung it at the disabled father, calling him a "useless old fart." The latter picked up the thin, broken pieces of glass with his trembling hands, looking quite helpless. Michiko stood by without a word and glared angrily at her brother. She felt like praying for his sudden death.

In the morning, Michiko would slowly open her eyes, hoping that Kanji was gone. When his large eyes, which were fixed on the ceiling, abruptly met hers, she sighed secretly with disappointment.

"How do you feel?" Michiko asked.

Kanji did not answer.

"You should be relaxed and easy-going. You're still young. Soon you'll get better, just wait and see. They say that the human body functions better when it's colder. You must stay alive."

"I'm not going to die. I've no intention of dying," said Kanji, defiantly, and looked at his sister with a slight, contemptuous smile. Michiko shuddered as she stole a glance at the patient's ashen face.

He pestered, "Buy me two eggs today." Even a small one cost twenty-two or twenty-three yen. He nonchalantly asked for things to eat: "Don't forget to buy the eggs. Buy me everything I ask for. . . ."

She seethed inside with rage.

The odor of the chamber pots used by the invalids filled the entire room and combined with the smell of creosol to produce a piercing stench. She could hardly stand it and wondered if there was any way out. From early morning, the din of the electric washing machine downstairs shook the mats on the second floor. Without changing this miserable state of affairs, neither she nor Emiko could go on living. Michiko prayed desperately for her younger brother's death.

When autumn came, Michiko followed Ranko's profession. She did not feel guilty. As the money accumulated, she hid the bills, stained by her own body, in her husband's bone box.

She bought a blanket on the black market. Now she could even buy a daily egg for Kanji. The patient picked up the egg with his wasted hand and held it up to the light, smiling broadly. Michiko was disgusted by the slight growth of moustache on her brother, who had not yet turned twenty. The high cheek bones, the sunken eyes, and the long hair which covered his ears made her cringe, being reminded of Hakaibo, the evil mendicant priest in a Kabuki play.

She dreaded the moment when she had to help him change his bedclothes, which were drenched with perspiration. Being accustomed to the responses of healthy males, she felt almost ill at the sight of her brother's unhealthy skin and protruding ribs. Once, when she held the urinal in front of him, she suddenly took a peek. A pathetic sight briefly held her eyes. "What an obstinate creature," she thought. Michiko could clearly see the incongruous symbol of his stubborn will to live, conspicuously outlined between his wasted thighs. "Ah, this boy is still trying to live on," she ruefully admitted to herself.

"Mother visits me quite often these days," said Kanji.

"She's probably watching over you," Michiko replied. "It won't be long now, eh?"

Her eyelids began to burn. "Why do you say that?"

"Because I feel funny sometimes...."

"You just lie there and think about foolish things, that's why. Why don't you ask mother for help?"

"You're right. I don't want to die....I *really* don't want to. Why is this happening to me?"

Michiko found no words to comfort him.

"I don't want to die. Who ever heard of somebody kicking off before his old man? You know, I read in the papers about 'ping pong therapy.' They say it helps if you put ping pong-size balls into the lungs to fill up the spaces. That kind of operation must be expensive...."

"Can they really do that?" she asked.

With his eyes blazing, Kanji looked directly at Michiko and said, "Can't you lend me that money?"

She blushed, stunned by this unexpected plea: How did he find out about the money hidden in the bone box?

"After the operation, I'll work and pay it all back when I'm strong again. I want to live. I don't want to die. I don't want to die *this way*." The pillow became soaked with his tears.

Michiko replied, "You want an operation? That won't be enough. You'd be lucky if you live on for two or three days longer. Suppose you have one, and it doesn't turn out right? Instead of risking that, you should eat all the things you like and take care of yourself."

"Hell, you don't give me enough to eat," snapped back Kanji. "The old man gets hold of everything and eats it by himself. That old fart! He tells me to hurry up and kick off. He's so tight, he won't even give me a cup of tea. Who can I depend on to take care of me? Emiko is the only one who shares anything. Still, don't you tell her not to get too close to me because she might catch T. B.? I'm going to give it to everybody!"

Throwing out all of Kanji's soiled things, Michiko retorted indignantly: "What are you talking about? You ....How do you think I'm feeding all of you every day? ....Well? Can't you tell that I'm miserable? You know ....if I wanted to, I could take Emiko right now and get out of here. I'm too soft toward both of you. Too soft ....I can't be a heartless monster. Even you can't understand why I can't be that way. You were born unlucky. Sooner or later, I'm going to be just like you, too.... That's why I'm in this filthy job, not caring a damn! You'd better curse the war rather than bite my head off. My husband died, too, didn't he? How am I to blame? 'I want an egg! Buy me an orange! Buy me an apple!'.... Don't I try my best to please you? Like a fool, you worked too hard at the factory. That's why you're sick now.

"You're the one who is stupid. Listen to me! Take my advice and go to a sanatorium or wherever you like. This time I'm really going to make the arrangements. You know it's useless!"

Kanji wailed loudly.

In the hallway, the father sat without a word in a broken wicker chair with Emiko, basking in the sun.

"I'm going to stay right here! It's better for me! If I'm going to die anyway, I want to stay here." Whimpering in a thin, hardly audible voice, Kanji begged like a child to be left where he was.

Kanji had been proud to do an honest day's work. He had always faced his job earnestly, fully convinced that Japan must be victorious. There had been nothing hypocritical in his behavior. And he could not understand why he was in such a bad way now when he had worked so hard. In his feverish dedication to work, he had been possessed with an unwavering spirit of patriotism. Whether awake or asleep, Kanji had never removed his headband with the Japanese flag and had worked as one with the machine. Even in the intense, dizzy heat of summer, he had never missed a day.

Her brother died one rainy morning in December. The father was not aware of it. Only the seven-year-old Emiko knew because he had turned cold.

Michiko returned at ten, after spending the night out. At the head of the bed, the father had thoughtfully placed a teacup filled with water and a pair of chopsticks wrapped around on one end with a thin strip of white cloth.

"Is he dead?" Michiko asked.

Then, she slowly made her way toward the bed and, kneeling, raised the soiled, purple wrapping cloth from the face of the corpse. While she stared at her brother's face, which had lost all sign of life, hysterical laughter began to well up in her throat. She virtually shouted as she shook the dead brother by the chest.

There was blood on his lips and nose; the lids were slightly open. In the foul-smelling air, only the area surrounding the dead body became steadily colder, as if a heavy object had been placed there.

"People say that Kan-chan choked to death on his own blood," explained Emiko, showing her the blood-soaked towel and dishpan.

"Didn't grandfather know?" asked Michiko.

"No," Emiko answered.

"He didn't even realize that his own son was dying!

That's why he's so stupid! Father, you're a. . . ."

The housewife next door, who sold fish on the black market, came in softly from the hallway to extend her sympathies. She said, "He was moaning for some reason during the night, but I thought it was the usual complaint and didn't bother to look in. I'm so sorry. . . ."

For the first time, Michiko felt compassion for Kanji's solitary death. Unloved by anyone, his brief existence was so pathetic. And she could hardly bear to see Kanji's arms, which had been folded on his breast by the father. She absentmindedly took hold of her brother's hands. How cold they were. She was overcome by a terrible feeling of guilt that plunged her into the very depths of hell.

Michiko was completely exhausted.

Suddenly she saw the baby buggy and the woman in the white apron. Feeling limp with fatigue, the cold hands of her brother felt soothing on her own feverish hands. Although it was repugnant to her, she still wanted to grasp Kanji's hands, even for this brief moment.

The woman next door said that she would return later to help and went down the stairs, carrying an empty fish basket.

It was pouring outside.

Michiko took down the bone box from the top of the tea cabinet and lifted the lid, thinking to herself that the money inside was, after all, meant for Kanji. On top of the red earth was the pile of dirty worn-out bills.

She placed a gauze, stained with lipstick, on Kanji's face. From time to time, the father soaked one end of a pair of chopsticks in the water and, lifting the gauze, moistened Kanji's lips.

The physician's report and the formalities at the ward office were completed. It was four days later that Kanji's cheap casket was carted away to the crematorium in Ochiai by a bicycle-drawn trailer.

The four-and-a-half mat dwelling became roomier. Standing in front of the signboard in front of the laundry, Michiko and Emiko looked on as the trailer passed through the alley, straddling the mud puddles. While she strained her ears to catch the sound of the trailer's rubber wheels, she carefully stored the white image of the cheap casket in her heart as it disappeared from the alley, swaying wildly from side to side.

Michiko tried to ease her guilty conscience by supposing that she, too, would eventually meet a similar fate. She cried bitterly, still standing in the road. A spot like a blackish lump flickered on and off in the laundry's window glass as it reflected the weak sunlight.

When Michiko went upstairs, her father was leaning over the window ledge. The stone used for pounding in the coffin nails had been left behind. She picked it up and placed it on top of her husband's bone box.

To Michiko, death was meaningless and even stupid.

Those destined to perish gradually disappeared from this world, completely helpless. But there was no other choice for people like herself. On the very night after her brother's coffin was sent away, she went out in the streets.

She simply lived in the present without knowing the reason why. Was it just bad luck? Then, how could human fate, predestined at birth, be so maliciously cruel? When she saw a beautiful, shining car or a smug woman in a fur coat, she felt unbearably jealous, as if her skin were pierced by a sharp sliver. She looked on in bewilderment. How could a class of people remain unperturbed despite the experience of that miserable war? Her own husband had been taken away and would never return.

Christmas would be here soon. All the pictures of Santa Claus in the children's books were designed to excite their hopes and desires. And Emiko believed implicitly in his existence.

On the third day after the casket had been taken away, Michiko took Emiko to the crematorium in Oshiai. Although he had been cremated at the cheapest price, Kanji's bones were already deposited in a funeral urn. Holding it close to her breast, Michiko walked in the balmy spring-like sun through the shanty town built on the site of the burned-out ruins. Emiko strolled beside her singing, "Jesus Loves Me," probably taught her by one of the neighbors. Michiko was trying to bear with the pain in her reeling head–the effect of the long ordeal.

The urn was heavier than she had expected.

A tattered baby buggy was left behind in front of the mat shop. Holding her daughter's hand, Michiko turned into the narrow alley. The smokestack of the crematorium was closer than she had realized and loomed up in front like a cross. The black smoke from the big chimney rose toward the blue sky.

Suddenly a thought crossed her mind: she wondered when her father would die.

Translated by Ted T. Takaya

Fumiko Hayashi was born in Shimonoseki on the southernmost tip of Honshu in 1904. Her stepfather being a traveling salesman, she was compelled to move with the family and transferred from school to school during her young days. She moved to Tokyo after graduating from high school and tried her hand at several different jobs. Her experiences were compiled in *Hōrōki* ("Diary of Roaming") in 1928-1930, and the work became a best seller. This book was referred to as "*lumpen* (vagrant's) literature" by some critics, but her lyric anarchism stood apart from proletarian writings. After two short-lived marriages, she married a painter and associated with anarchist writers, but continued to write autobiographical novels throughout the 1930's. She was awarded the Women Writer's Award for her *Bangiku* ("Late Chrysanthemum") in 1948, a short story which pursued the heights of realism. "Bones" was published in 1949 and remains as one of her representative short stories. She died suddenly in 1951 while writing *Meshi* ("Rice"). She also wrote poetry and children's stories.

Mirror, Sword and Jewel 日本人とはなにか by Kurt Singer

The Doctor's Wife 華岡青洲の妻 by Sawako Ariyoshi

Lou-lan 楼蘭 by Yasushi Inoue

The Silent Cry 万延元年のフットボール by Kenzaburō Ōe

Japanese Religion 日本の宗教 by the Agency for Cultural Affairs

Appreciations of Japanese Culture 日本文化論 by Donald Keene

Almost Transparent Blue 限りなく透明に近いブルー by Ryū Murakami

Clara's Diary クララの日記 by Clara Whitney

The Day Man Lost 原爆の落ちた日 by The Pacific War Research Society